A Spectral Presence

The moon went behind a cloud, and its silver radiance dulled to pewter, but there was still enough light to see the white figure dimly before me. It swerved and left the pavement for the lawn between the pool and the garden. Then it disappeared. Not suddenly, but in slow motion, like the melting of a candle. The slender figure about the height of an average-size woman sank slowly earthward, growing shorter and shorter until there was nothing left but a small blob of white on on the ground.

We will send you a free catalog on request. Any titles not in your local book store can be purchased by mail. Send the price of the book plus 35c shipping charge to Belmont Tower Books, Two Park Avenue, New York, New York 10016.

Titles currently in print are available in quantity for industrial and sales promotion use at reduced rates. Address inquiries to our Promotion Department.

GHOST AT THE WEDDING

Elna Stone

BELMONT TOWER BOOKS • NEW YORK CITY

A BELMONT TOWER BOOK

Published by
Tower Publications, Inc.
Two Park Avenue
New York, N.Y. 10016

Copyright © MCMLXXI by Tower Publications, Inc.
All rights reserved

PRINTED IN THE UNITED STATES OF AMERICA

Chapter 1

As soon as we turned off the highway, sunlit pastures patched with still brown ponds and herds of black cattle disappeared, and thick woods surrounded us, hemmed us in, reaching even into the narrow road to brush the car with grasping green fingers. Trees and bushes pushed against each other, fighting for growing space, and vines as thick as my arm grew up into the trees and twisted among the branches searching for sunlight. Accustomed only to paved streets, clipped hedges, and orderly flower beds, I found this country wild and threatening, different from the drowsy, fragrant place I had pictured when Alex spoke of Wisteria, the Mississippi plantation which was his home.

We topped a low hill, and below us was a narrow

wooden bridge, not wide enough, I thought, for a car. I looked at Alex, but behind their dark glasses his eyes looked straight ahead, and his face had a preoccupied, absentminded expression. He was used to the rough road, the dangerous bridges, the wild dark woods; this country was his home, and he saw nothing strange or sinister in it. As we rattled across the loose boards of the bridge, I looked down at the brown, turbid water.

Suddenly the car swerved. The wheels spun perilously close to the dropoff, and I gasped. With a muttered oath Alex got back to the center of the road.

"Sorry," he said. "I didn't want to hit that snake with the car windows down. Even the severed head of a cottonmouth can bite with enough venom to kill."

I shuddered at the picture his words brought, and the shudder did not stop as the snake was left behind. The May sunshine was warm, but I felt cold inside. Dread and fear were freezing my happiness, taking away the confidence I had fought so hard to gain. The prayer I had made up when I was a child flashed into my mind: "This is Tracy Meadows, God. Please make me bright and good and pretty, and let somebody love me."

Now at last it had come true. Perhaps I was not quite all I had hoped. I wasn't pretty, and I never would be, but the strange combination of light brown hair, dark skin, and jade green eyes gave me a certain distinction. I was bright enough to have graduated from college with honors two years before when I was twenty. And Alex loved me. We would be married next week, and I would never be alone again.

I had been lonely all my life. My parents were killed in a plane crash when I was seven, and I was not the kind of child who attracts attention. If I'd had looks or talent, or even if I had been a problem child, it might have been different; a teacher or other adult might have noticed me and realized my needs. But plain and quiet and studious, I was lost in the shuffle at the expensive private school I attended. I had only Grandfather, and he was always half a world away looking after his mining interests.

But now I had Alex. I looked at him again, but his eyes were still on the road ahead. A small muscle twitched in his jaw. Fascinated, I watched it, wondering if it was involuntary or if he was doing something to cause it. Clenching and unclenching his teeth perhaps. That would mean he was as tense as I was. Or Perhaps he was holding back a smile. What would that mean? I knew so little about this man who was soon to be my husband.

But, I told myself firmly, I loved him, and what more did I need to know? It wasn't Alex who was making me nervous; it was the others, the members of his family. Would they like me? Would I fit in? Since the age of seven I had known only Miss Blaine's Academy, Okewanna Summer Camp, and Belmont Presbyterian College. I had had no experience with meeting strangers or adapting myself to different surroundings. Even after graduation I stayed on at the college to work as a librarian, thinking myself lucky to find a good job without having to leave the place which had become home to me. It was only after the first year that I had begun to feel the dullness of my existence. Was this what I had waited for all those lonely years? Were orderly files and a polished brass nameplate on my desk to be the sum of my life?

Then one dark winter day Alex came striding purposefully toward my desk, his neat business suit looking out of place among the sweaters and jackets of the college boys. Seeing his dark, stern face, I thought, Oh, dear, a new professor, and he's going to be impatient.

But he waited his turn politely, and his voice was deep and pleasant as he told me what he wanted, a look at the files of an old newspaper. He was doing the research for a history of his family, and having heard we had the complete files of several country newspapers, he decided to check while he was in town on business. I explained that our newspapers were on microfilm and went to show him how to work the machine.

That was only three months ago, and now here I was on my way to Wisteria, his family home, to marry him.

"Now that you've said yes, I'd like to get married quickly," he had said last week. "I've waited long enough. Forty—how ancient that must seem to you. Are you sure you want to marry someone so much older?"

I laughed at his foolishness. I never thought of the difference in our ages. I could talk to him in a way I never could with boys my own age whose speech seemed to consist of zippy comments I couldn't follow, much less return. Talking to them was like learning a foreign language, except that as soon as I found out what the words meant, they were out of style. But I could speak Alex's language, and I shared many of his interests. The hours sped by when we were together, and I lived from one date to another.

Once when I was talking to him then, I stopped, suddenly conscious that I was chattering, telling him the details of my life.

"Go on," he said.

"I'm talking too much. I don't want to bore you."

"You could never do that. I want to know everything about you. I feel very possessive about you."

I frowned and moved restlessly on the car seat. I wanted Alex to be possessive. I wanted our relationship to be just between the two of us.

I snapped out of my reverie as Alex braked suddenly for a sharp curve ahead. I realized that we must be very close to Wisteria. I had been nervous and depressed all morning, and now, with the imminence of arrival, I felt an overwhelming premonition of disaster. These dark tangled woods, the snake which seemed a precursor of evil, Alex's preoccupied silence, all seemed to tell me I was right in not wanting to come to Wisteria to be married.

It was Alex's suggestion that we have the wedding at his home. "Your grandfather can come to Wisteria as easily as here, and my family would already be there," he said. "Maybe it isn't customary, but it would be a lot more convenient. Myra would love helping you with the arrangements. Besides," he added, "I don't want to spend another week without you. I waited half a lifetime to find you, and I want you with me every day from now on."

When he put it that way, how could I refuse?

But now I wished we had planned it differently. If we had got married first, if I had come to Wisteria as Mrs. Alex Farrington, I wouldn't be so nervous. It wouldn't seem as if I were being presented for approval. It would have had to be a hurried wedding without preparation, but we could have done it this morning in the time it took to make our wills.

Perhaps making the wills was at the bottom of my fear and depression. It was sweet and practical of Alex to think of it, but it brought melancholy thoughts. I didn't want to think of endings when life was just beginning.

I moved a little closer to Alex and asked, "How much farther is it?"

"No farther," he said, making a right turn. "There it is."

The house was beautiful; there was no denying that. Standing well back from the road on a slight rise, it was big and square with white columns and red brick chimneys, a perfect example of the neoclassical architecture of the antebellum South. Yet its symmetry and grace, its fresh paint and shining windows oppressed me; they were like the powder and rouge on a corpse, hiding putrescence. And wisteria drooped over everything like a lavender shroud. It was up and down the fences on each side of the house, on trellises, pruned into bushes, even covering the top of a tall pine tree. The lavender blossoms had a silvery shine; they fell silently over the whole landscape, like luminescent tears. A wave of heavy scent, a sweetness with decay at its heart, came on the warm breeze, and I was for a moment back at my parents' funeral, smelling the cloying fragrance of the flowers, hearing the mournful organ music, feeling the dark despair of the desolate.

Mentally, I shook myself and looked back at the house. Above that drooping mass of lavender, it stood cold and silent, offering no welcome, its blank face staring at me with cold malice. Icy fingers tightened around my heart; I knew I was not going to be happy here.

But that was only imagination, bride's nerves. A house had no life or personality of its own; it merely reflected the people who lived in it. I loved Alex, and I would like the others, too. When I felt more at home, Wisteria would look different to me.

At least the sun is shining, I thought. Happy the bride the sun shines on. But at that moment it went behind a cloud; the shining paint on the house darkened; the lavender flowers dulled to gray, and the dark cedars stood like black-clad mourners on either side of the steps.

We swept up the long drive and turned left to stop in front of the wide white-columned porch. Just then the front door opened, and a girl about my own age came out. She had lovely, clear brown eyes, but her blue dress was too fussy, her hair too elaborately dressed, her makeup too heavy. She reminded me of a little girl who has put on her mother's clothes and cosmetics.

She opened the car door for me and said, "I'm so glad to meet you at last, Tracy. How nice that you made it just at lunch time. We were hoping you would; everyone is here to meet you. I'm Pam, Alex's niece. And here's Britt, my brother," she added as a tall blond boy came up behind her. At least I thought of him as a boy, although he was probably a year or two older than I was. But beside Alex, his handsome face looked like a half-finished portrait with all the lines of personality and character missing. I thought there was a look of surprise in his blue eyes as he said, "Welcome to Wisteria, Tracy." He turned quickly to Alex. "Can I help with the luggage?"

I felt better after their friendly greetings. Perhaps I was wrong about Wisteria. Perhaps after all everything would be fine.

While they got out my suitcases, Pam and I walked into the house. The front door opened into an enormous—hallway? It was an expanse of polished oak flooring running the length of the house. The grand piano, an elaborate sideboard, and a few chairs and tables along each side hardly broke into the space. Doors opened off it on each side, and at the far end was a wide staircase.

"This is the ballroom," Pam said. "We still have dances here sometimes, but mostly it's just a hall. The sideboard is a bar, in case you're ever in need of fortification. Let's go into the living room. Chris, my husband, has made martinis, although of course he can't drink at lunch time."

"Why not?"

"His patients would disapprove. There is an awful lot of opposition to alcohol around here, and Chris is still on probation. No one is quite sure he can fill Dr. Manning's shoes."

The living room was filled with beautiful antique furniture, but even here one could not get away from the wisteria. The triple windows framed a view of the bushes on the lawn outside, and great masses of the flowers were placed throughout the room. The blues and purples of the color scheme seemed designed to compliment the lavender blossoms.

A short square-built man wearing glasses and a plain sallow girl in a yellow dress came forward to meet us.

"This is Chris," Pam said. "And Sandra Parker, Britt's—"

As she hesitated, Sandra drawled. "Let's try fiancé. It isn't official yet, but I'm working on it."

"Don't let her kid you," Pam said. "She has Britt in the palm of her hand. They've been steadies since high school."

I was saved the necessity of commenting by the entrance of the most beautiful woman I had ever seen. Shining blond hair, cornflower blue eyes, and a flawless complexion were set off by a blue dress the exact color of her eyes and muted makeup that seemed merely to allow her natural beauty to shine through. She came forward with outstretched hands. "Tracy, how nice of you to come. I'm Myra."

Myra? She couldn't be Alex's sister-in-law, the

widow of his older brother, Roy Farrington. "Myra is a marvel of efficiency," Alex had said. "She runs Wisteria with one hand and the town of Abbeville with the other. She brought up Roy's children just as if they were her own, and they are both crazy about her."

So naturally I had pictured a plump, middle-aged woman with the genius for organization that mothers often seem to have, or acquire. Never in my wildest imagination could I have come up with Myra as she really was, slim and lovely, looking hardly out of her twenties. Although if she had brought up Pam and Britt, she couldn't be far from forty.

I must have showed my surprise, because Myra laughed and said, "Everyone says I look more like Pam's sister than her stepmother."

"I wouldn't have believed it," I said honestly. "You're so much younger than I imagined."

"That Alex! He isn't to be depended on for descriptions. You aren't at all what I expected either." But she didn't say what she thought I would be like.

She turned to Pam. Suddenly, I saw why I had thought Pam overdressed and too made up. She had tried to copy Myra's style, not realizing that Myra's precise perfection didn't suit her at all.

"Pam, you thoughtless girl, get Tracy a martini," Myra said.

"No thank you. I don't care for one," I said.

"Would you rather have something else? A glass of sherry perhaps?"

"Oh, no," I said hastily, realizing she thought I

was being choosy. "I really shouldn't drink anything."

A tiny frown appeared on her face. "Not even one while we get acquainted?"

I thought perhaps I had offended her by refusing what she offered me. Yet I didn't want to drink. I wasn't accustomed to it for one thing; the college had strict rules, and it had never occurred to me to break them. Also, I had been too nervous to eat breakfast this morning, and I had heard that one could get drunk quickly on an empty stomach. But how could I tell Myra any of that without sounding like a child?

So I took the drink Pam offered and sipped it cautiously, determined not to gag and choke. I was surprised to find that it didn't burn at all and had quite a pleasant taste.

Myra was talking to me, asking polite, interested questions about my job and my former life. None of the others said very much. Even Pam, who had chattered away until Myra came into the room, sat quietly on the sofa and stared at the drink she held in her hand. Chris smoked and looked at Pam. Sandra moved to the window and stood looking out, her back to us. I was feeling more relaxed now and talked along easily, telling Myra about our plans, Alex's and mine.

"Alex said it would be best to have the wedding here. I hope you don't mind. It shouldn't be much trouble; I thought we would have a simple ceremony with just the family present. Grandfather will come, of course, but he can stay at a hotel as he always does when he visits me."

"Of course we can't let him stay at a hotel," Myra said. "My goodness, one guest is nothing at Wisteria. We've had dozens, haven't we, Pam? And we would love helping you with the wedding. Pam didn't have one herself, but she has been in several and knows how it's done."

A dull red flush spread over Pam's face and neck. Chris said, "Oh, we're married. What Myra means is that we eloped instead of having a big wedding."

Pam said lightly, breaking a little silence I found uncomfortable, "I'll make a bargain with you, Tracy. I'll help with your wedding if you'll help with my house hunt."

"House hunt?"

"Chris and I aren't permanent residents; we're just staying at Wisteria until we find a place of our own."

"We've been looking a year now," Chris said dryly.

"You know you're welcome to stay here," Myra said. "I like having my family around me. It's foolish for you to move into some little box of a house when we have this lovely big one with room enough for everyone."

"Perhaps Tracy will want her house to herself," Chris said. He looked at me, but I thought he was talking to Myra, perhaps reminding her that soon I would be mistress of Wisteria. Again I was uncomfortable, feeling that there were tensions here I did not understand. I couldn't think what to say, and I felt my face redden. Should I assure them I meant to make no changes? But perhaps even that would be a presumption.

I was still hesitating when Alex and Britt came in. Myra again asked Pam to bring the drinks.

"None for me," Alex said.

"If you say so," Myra said. "Tracy and I will have one more." She didn't leave any room for refusal. This would be my third, but I wasn't feeling any effect at all, so I was sure it was all right.

"Shall we eat?" Myra said later, when there was a lull in the conversation. I looked down at my glass and was surprised to find it still half full. I drank the rest quickly and set the glass down. When I got up, the room swung around. I closed my eyes. When I opened them, the room was still, but my head seemed to be spinning. I took a careful step and knocked against a chair. I apologized and moved unsteadily aside. Alex took my elbow. "How much have you had to drink?" he asked.

Suddenly sweat popped out on my forehead, and my stomach turned over. "I feel sick," I gasped.

I was vaguely conscious of Alex and Pam hurrying me down the hall and into a bathroom. Later, someone—still Pam, I guess—helped me to bed.

Chapter 2

When I woke, it was three o'clock. For a moment I couldn't imagine where I was or why, but soon it all came back, and I felt sick all over again. What must they think of me? How humiliated Alex must have been. I would have liked to stay in bed, pretend I was really sick, not have to face any of them. But of course I couldn't do that. I must apologize.

I took aspirin for my headache and then showered and dressed. When I got my makeup on, I thought no one could know that underneath it I was white-faced or that my head was still pounding in spite of the aspirin. I went downstairs and started toward the living room. Alex came to the door of a room on the left. "I've been waiting for you to wake," he said. "How do you feel?"

"Fine. Oh, Alex, I'm so sorry. I wanted so much to make a good impression, and then to do a dumb thing like that."

He frowned. "I don't understand it. I thought you didn't drink."

Should I tell him how Myra had urged me? But she was only being hospitable; the trouble was that I hadn't known how to refuse gracefully. It was my fault.

"I suppose not being used to it was why it hit me so hard. That and not eating anything this morning. Anyway, I'm sorry. I wouldn't have embarrassed you for the world."

"It did rather spoil the luncheon Myra had worked on so hard," he said.

I blinked back threatening tears. "I'm sorry," I said again.

"Forget it," he said. But his voice was cool.

"No, not until I apologize to the others."

"You'll have to wait for that. Pam is out house hunting, and Myra has gone off somewhere. She left a tray for you on the buffet in the dining room. After you eat, I thought I would show you the house if you feel up to it."

So apparently he had forgiven me. I was humbly grateful, eager to please. Disregarding my headache, I said, "I'd love to see the house. The part I've already seen is beautiful." I realized, however, that I had hardly noticed the bedroom I was in, being so worried about the poor impression I had made.

In my interest in the house, I forgot about my headache. Downstairs, besides the living room, dining room, and ballroom, there was a library and Alex's office. The furniture was old and beautifully kept, mostly Victorian, although there were a few pieces of Chippendale and Sheraton. The library was a cozy, book-lined room with crimson velvet furnishings; Alex's office was brown leather and yellow linen with touches of orange.

"This room had to be completely refurnished," Alex said. "It hadn't been used for an office since the early days, and all the furniture had disappeared. But Myra shopped the auctions and antique shops and redid it."

"It's lovely," I said. "There's a desk exactly like that in the President's Mansion at the college. I wonder if yours—" I suddenly caught back my words. I had been going to say—I wonder if yours has a secret drawer. But perhaps Alex would consider that an invasion of privacy. I didn't want to make any more mistakes. So I said instead: "I wonder if yours is mahogany, too," although I could see plainly that it was.

The upstairs hall was lined with pictures that were obviously family portraits. Many were enlarged photographs in ornate gold frames, but there were some paintings, too. Alex stopped before a large full-figure oil portrait of a man in a Confederate uniform. "My great-great-grandfather, the first master of Wisteria," he said.

I felt I could have looked at the picture for hours, but Alex was passing on, so I hurried after him. He didn't say who any of the others were, and, determined to let him show me everything in his own way and his own time, I didn't ask. There would be plenty of time to learn the things I wanted to know.

Alex was crossing and recrossing the hall, opening doors on each side to show me the bedrooms. I saw four-poster beds, beds with high carved headboards, sleigh beds, spool beds—a mixture of styles and periods. Yet in each room the pieces had been carefully chosen to complement each other and to reflect the personality of the occupant. Thus Alex's room was heavy and masculine, filled with marble-topped pieces with great mirrors, while Myra's was graceful and delicate with cream-colored Louis XV furniture and floral-patterned fabrics.

"It's beautiful," I said for the hundredth time.

"It was pretty much of a hodge-podge before Myra came," he said. "Every generation had moved some of the old furniture into the carriage house and bought whatever happened to be in style. But Myra brought back a lot of it and put things together the way they are now—at considerable expense of course."

But in spite of his wry tone I could see that he was very proud of the house. Myra had done it very well. Apparently Alex's praise of her efficiency was deserved.

At the end of the hall, I stopped before a pastel portrait of a young girl. It was a fairly modern picture; the girl had dark shoulder-length hair and wore a yellow skirt and sweater. She was looking sideways with an expectant smile, as if she were waiting for something or someone.

"Who is this?" I asked, thinking perhaps she might be Pam's and Britt's mother, Roy's first wife. But Alex, opening the double doors at the end of the hall, apparently didn't hear my question. I asked again.

"Her name was Elizabeth," he said. "Come look at the view from here."

I went on the balcony and looked across the wide lawn, framed by the sad, drooping wisteria blossoms. Alex took my hand and said, "Wisteria has some unhappy memories for me, but I love it, and I hope you will, too. I think we can fill this house so full of love there won't be room for anything else."

We left the balcony and went back down the hall. Alex stopped at the head of the stairs and turned me to face the double windows looking toward the back of the house.

"The sun deck is built on the roof of the kitchen," he said, pointing to the left. "I don't know whether you noticed, but it opens off your room. There are stairs up to it from the terrace."

I hadn't noticed, but I hardly looked at the sun deck, because something else caught my eye. "You have a garden," I said.

"Not very well tended, but I hope to get it back in shape some day."

"Could I do it?" I asked eagerly. "I don't know much about gardening, but I could learn." I thought if I put something of myself into Wisteria, it would begin to seem like home. Everything else was already done, and done so beautifully, anything more would be superfluous. The garden was my only chance.

"Well, I don't know," he said slowly. "There has been so much expense—Myra's decorating has been a drain for years, and the swimming pool she wanted this spring isn't paid for yet."

I suppose he saw the question on my face, because he said, "Roy was the oldest, but the house and land were left to me, since he didn't like farming and I did. So I pay for whatever improvements are made. Roy got the business, a chain now called Roy's Top Value Stores. Roy was a pretty good businessman, but in the last few years he expanded too rapidly, and the business was in pretty bad shape when he died. Britt bought out Myra—Pam gave him her share—and I've lent him some money and most of my time for the past year trying to get it back on it's feet. What I'm saying is that right now I'm not as prosperous as I look. Things will straighten out soon, but the garden may have to wait awhile."

"I'll spend my own money," I said. "You wouldn't mind that, would you? After all, when we're married, it will be yours, too."

He said in a teasing voice, "I don't mind how you spend your money. But don't you think you ought to keep your little nest egg for mad money? You may get tired of me one of these days."

I laughed and took his hand, feeling close to him for the first time since coming to Wisteria. I said, "It's more than a little nest egg, Alex. My parents had some property, and then they bought flight insurance before they left on that fatal plane trip. I got quite a lot of money, and Grandfather has increased it through the years."

"How much do you have?"

"Almost half a million dollars."

His black eyes stared at me unbelievingly. "My God," he said at last. "Why didn't you tell me?"

I looked out over the garden, refusing to meet his eyes.

"There was a boy when I was in college—it turned out he was only after my money."

He frowned. "You didn't tell me about anyone else."

"I didn't see any reason to. It was three years ago."

"Three years isn't that long. Are you still in love with him?"

"Of course I'm not still in love with him. I don't think I ever was. It was mostly moonglow, my own romantic imaginings. But at the time, the breakup was quite painful."

The expression on his face changed him, made him ugly. I said urgently, "Don't you see why I didn't tell you? I had to be sure it was me you wanted and not my money."

He started to say something else, then caught it back. The anger on his face disappeared. "Yes, I see." He kissed me lightly on the forehead. "I'll just have to get used to the idea of being married to a rich girl. And to answer your question, of course you can spend your money to redo the garden if you want to. Would you like to look at it now?"

But we didn't, because when we got back downstairs, Myra was back. I apologized for my disgraceful behavior at lunch, and she said, "It was partly my fault for not realizing how young and inexperienced you are and partly Alex's for not watching over you better." I wondered if Alex realized how her gracious-sounding words separated us, putting him in her adult world and me in a category of children needing watching. I was beginning to dislike Myra.

She said to me, "Did you get unpacked yet? But of course not; there's been no time. I'd better show you the closet space."

We went upstairs to my room, and she pulled back the blue striped draperies that entirely covered one outside wall of the room, revealing clothes rods between the three windows.

"I think you'll find everything you need. If not, just say so. I want you to be happy here. As long as you can," she finished half under her breath.

"What do you mean?" I asked quickly.

"Nothing. No, really, I didn't mean anything."

I said in a cool voice, "You said I was to be happy as long as I could. I want to know what you meant."

"Perhaps I'm wrong. Perhaps you can accept"—she hesitated a moment—"traditions better than I. Thank goodness, the question never came up between Roy and me. But then he didn't hold to tradition the way Alex does. And anyway, he wasn't the master of Wisteria."

"Alex is interested in history," I agreed. "That's how we met. But I don't see what it has to do with my being happy here."

"Don't tell me he hasn't told you! Really, he should have. It isn't fair to let you face it, not knowing."

"Face what?"

"The mark of the Farringtons."

"I don't know what you're talking about."

"Well, it isn't my place to tell you," she said. "Ask Alex. He certainly owes you an explanation before the wedding." She looked at her watch and said briskly, "I must see about dinner. Dinner is at seven-thirty, but it won't hurt if you're a few minutes late. We're pretty informal, and Mrs. Gilbert is seldom on time."

I put her puzzling remarks out of my mind and unpacked. When I finally finished, I realized I had just time to slip into a fresh dress. I was giving my hair a final brush when someone knocked on my door.

It was Pam, wearing a long blue evening dress. She said, "I came in to borrow some blue eye shadow."

"It's a good thing you did. I didn't realize you dressed for dinner," I said.

"We don't usually, but we're having guests tonight. I guess Myra forgot to tell you."

"Yes, she did. But it won't take long to change." I whipped off the short white dress and jerked a green crepe and chiffon evening dress off its hanger. It was new and had packed beautifully, so it didn't need pressing. I was already wearing a black velvet choker with my grandmother's cameo pinned to it, so I didn't even have to worry about more jewelry. I was ready in two minutes.

27

We turned to go, and I said, "You forgot the eye shadow." Then I looked closely at her and realized she was already wearing some. But she went through the motions of using mine.

"How lucky you can dress so quickly," she said. "It's quite a *faux pas* around here to be late for dinner. We'll have missed the cocktails as it is. I waited and waited to hear you go down—my room is next door—and when I didn't, I thought I'd better come and see."

As we went into the hall, Pam chattered on. "It's no wonder Myra forgot to tell you with all she has on her mind. It isn't easy to give a dinner party here. Mrs. Gilbert doesn't like extra work, so Myra has to keep her smoothed down and see that the girls—Kay and Linda, Mrs. Gilbert's teen-aged daughters—know how to serve. Somehow Myra always manages to have everything under control. She's really a marvel."

I was getting a bit tired of hearing how wonderful Myra was, but I said, "It's nice that you get along so well. People often don't with stepmothers."

"There's none of that with us. Britt and I owe her so much. And she was so good to Daddy, never lost her sense of humor, no matter how he embarrassed her. I guess you know he was an alcoholic. But really a wonderful person, always kind and gentle even when he was drinking."

By that time we had reached the living room. It seemed full of people, but I saw Myra immediately. She was wearing a dress of smoky blue with some spectacular diamonds in her ears and around her delicate wrists. Her eyes narrowed momentarily when she saw me, and for a moment I wondered if there was something wrong with my appearance after all.

Myra's displeasure—if such it was—was quickly over. "Here's our guest of honor," she said, taking my hand and beginning to introduce me to the people nearby. "I'm sorry you're too late for a drink, my dear," she said to me, "but perhaps it's just as well after what happened at noon. It was the most embarrassing thing," she said to the plump, pink-clad woman on her right. "Alex hadn't told me Tracy didn't drink and—well, we got her drunk. Just a couple of martinis, but she had to go to bed and miss lunch."

Then to another person she said, "Here's Alex's child bride. Isn't she lovely?" I smiled and murmured something, wondering if Myra's mixture of insults and compliments was deliberate or accidental. Child bride indeed! I was twenty-two years old.

I met other people, uttered polite, empty remarks.

At dinner, Myra sat at one end of the table and Alex at the other. I was on Myra's right. But soon I would sit in her chair; I would be the hostess at Wisteria. I wondered uneasily how I should manage. Probably not as well as Myra, who had been doing it for years.

Suddenly I realized that my marriage to Alex was making almost as many changes for Myra as it was for me. Perhaps that was why she seemed—a bit hostile. The thought brought me a new sympathy and understanding, made me determined to overlook Myra's seeming antagonism, ask her advice about things, make the change as easy for her as possible.

I tried to talk to the bald man on my right, but he seemed to be deaf. He had to ask me to repeat everything, and even then his expression was puzzled and dissatisfied as he tried to answer a remark imperfectly understood. I wondered if I was embarrassing him by my efforts to talk, and finally I gave up and sat silently, listening to the murmuring sounds as conversation rose and fell in little waves up and down the table. Myra was talking to the man on her left, but after a time she turned to me, "We're going to dance afterward," she said. "You *do* dance, don't you?"

"Yes," I replied.

"I didn't know. Young people of today seem to have so few of the social graces."

I said evenly, "I also play bridge, swim, ride horseback, ice skate, ski, and play the piano. But I think social grace is a matter of making people feel at ease, rather than a list of performances." As soon as I said it, I was ashamed of myself. I had just resolved to understand Myra, and here I was being as insulting to her as she had been to me all evening.

She looked at me a moment. Then she said with a smile, "I'm afraid we can't offer ice skating and skiing. But the other things are available, and several people are entertaining for you. There are two bridal showers, I think, and a couple of parties. We'll go over the schedule tomorrow."

I could feel my blush hot on my face. Had she really thought I was demanding entertainment?

Afterward, when we were dancing in the ballroom, I said, "Alex, why does Myra dislike me?"

He drew back, looking startled. "What makes you think she does? Has she said something?"

"No," I said slowly. There was nothing I could tell him without sounding young and petulant. Still, something about Myra's attitude troubled me. I asked, "What is the mark of the Farringtons?"

I could feel his arm tense, and his face looked dark with anger. But after a moment he said carelessly, "Oh, you mean a trademark? A wisteria bloom, of course. I use it on the letterheads and farm trucks."

"What does it have to do with me?"

"Nothing that I know of. Why?"

"Myra seemed to think it did."

He missed a step and said, "Look, I can talk or I can dance, but I can't do both. So let's dance."

"No, let's talk."

"All right," he said reluctantly. We were near the back of the ballroom, and Alex guided me through the double doors and down the brick steps to the terrace. No one else was here. We sat down and Alex said, "Now, what did you want to talk about?"

"The mark of the Farringtons."

"Oh, that. You don't want to hear about it, Tracy. It's an old legend I wish everybody would forget. I don't like it mentioned even as a joke."

31

"If it's only a joke, surely you don't mind telling me."

"Oh, all right, have it your own way. It is unpleasant, but it doesn't take long to tell. There's a tradition that the master of Wisteria and his bride make a pact on their wedding night that goes beyond the marriage ceremony. They promise to be faithful to eternity."

"Not just till death?" I asked slowly.

"Not just till death. To eternity. It would mean, you see, not only fidelity to their marriage vows but also that neither of them could ever marry again."

"That's a strange way to refer to a promise," I said. "Calling it the mark of the Farringtons."

"The mark of the Farringtons is not the promise. It's the way the promise is sealed."

Something dark and fearful had come to crouch on the terrace, some nameless horror I could only guess at from his words. "How?" I whispered.

"With a branding iron," he said. "Supposedly, the master of Wisteria burns the wisteria design on his bride's skin."

So now the horror had a name. And a home in my mind. Its monstrous tentacles took hold of my brain, squeezing out every vision but one lurid picture of a red-hot iron above white skin. Then a quick thrust, the searing pain, the scream of agony, the sickening odor of charred flesh. I made a retching sound, and Alex caught my shoulder, shook me roughly. "I told you it was unpleasant," he said harshly. "It's also untrue. Can you imagine my doing a thing like that?"

I suppose I should have laughed, showed him how ridiculous such a story was in this modern day. But somehow I couldn't. I was thinking of Alex's possessiveness. Thinking of his anger this afternoon when I told him about that long-ago college boy. I knew there were dark depths in Alex, depths which I had only glimpsed once or twice. If the mark of the Farringtons were only an unpleasant joke, why was he so reluctant to tell me the story? The trouble was that I didn't know him well enough. "Can you imagine my doing a thing like that?" he had asked. No, I couldn't imagine it. But I could imagine a time when it would be possible to imagine it.

Alex was talking again. "I said there's no truth in the story, and there isn't—now. But there may have been once. In my research I've come across a couple of references that sound as if old Alexander Rufus Farrington, the man whose portrait you saw this afternoon, might have done some such thing. He was a slaveowner, a rather cruel one, I'm afraid. Times were different then. No matter what kind of romantic stories they tell about the old South, there were a lot of ugly things going on beneath the surface graciousness.

"Anyway," he finished, "that story isn't important. But something else is. Something I should have told you long ago. I'd better do it now before someone else does. I've been married before, Tracy."

I stared at him in the dim light coming through the doors from the ballroom, but his face was only a white blur; I couldn't discern his expression.

Married! He had been married, and he had never told me.

"What happened?" I asked when I could find my voice.

"She died."

Chapter 3

His words jumped around in my mind like the letters on a flashing neon sign. One minute I would seem to have hold of them; the next moment they would blink out, leaving only blackness. "Why didn't you tell me?" I cried.

"Because I was afraid you would take it like this."

"Like what? How should I take it? You can't wait until a week before the wedding to tell me it's your second marriage and expect me not to ask any questions."

At length I said, "Aren't you going to tell me about your marriage? When did your wife die? What was she like? Did you have any children?" For a moment I wondered if my voice was too high.

Alex picked up my last question and answered roughly, "Of course not. Don't you think I'd have told you if there had been children?"

"I don't know. You forgot to mention a wife." I could hear resentment tightening my voice, making it harsh and angry.

"I didn't forget it. I didn't tell you because I didn't see any reason to."

I stared at his face, trying to see it in the dim light, trying to read his expression, because I couldn't believe I heard his words correctly. There must be some explanation in his eyes or the set of his mouth; there had to be something that wasn't getting through to me. He couldn't be saying there was no reason to tell me about his first marriage. Me, the girl he was going to marry!

But he was still talking, looking not at me but toward the shadowy garden. "I don't go around telling everyone I meet the story of my life," he said.

"I'm not everyone you meet," I cried.

"Not now. But at first you were just an attractive girl I met in a library, nice to spend a few hours with in a strange town. I had no notion of seeing you again. And sometimes I think it would have been better if I hadn't. Maybe if you knew me better, you would think so, too."

"Why did you see me again?" I asked. My words hung between us, saying more than their meaning, saying I wish you hadn't. For a moment I did wish it. I wished I had never heard of Alex Farrington, had never come to this godforsaken spot to marry him. I wished I could be back in the college library, wrapped inside my dull routine so that pain could never touch me.

He repeated my question. "Why did I see you again?" I don't think he actually shrugged, but the gesture was in his voice as he said, "I had to come back on business the following week."

"And not having anything better to do, you called me." I got up and walked to the edge of the terrace. It was darker here; he couldn't see my face. "Why did you want to marry me?" I asked.

His head jerked up sharply, and his voice sounded startled. "Good Lord, what kind of question is that?"

"A reasonable one, I think. You've just said you only took me out because you had nothing better to do. Did you decide to marry me for the same reason?"

"Don't be silly. How did we get into this anyway? I was only trying to tell you about my first marriage, and you've made a quarrel out of it. I wish I hadn't brought it up. It has nothing to do with us."

"Nothing to do with us! It has everything to do with us. It changes the way I have to think of you, makes you a different person with a set of experiences I never guessed at."

"There's nothing to guess. I'll tell you about it, if you'll only give me a chance. It was fifteen years ago when I was twenty-five," he said in a rapid, expressionless voice. "I had finished college and served my time in the army, and I came home ready to settle down and get on with life. Elizabeth —Elizabeth Lavelle—lived in Abbeville, but she was six years younger than I, so she had grown up while I was away. She was very beautiful and—attracted to me. We were married a few months after I came home, and she died a year later. The picture you asked about upstairs is a portrait of her."

"Why didn't you tell me when I asked about the picture? Why did you say 'Her name was Elizabeth,' and change the subject?"

"If I had told you who she was, you would have stood there looking at the picture and asking questions. I would have had to look at it, too. I didn't want to do that."

Pain clutched at my heart, pain for myself, pain for him, pain for the girl who had died so young, loving Alex. Now I could understand why he didn't tell me about his marriage; it was because it hurt him to talk about her. Even now he hurried through the explanation, skirting emotion, keeping to facts. He couldn't bear even to look at her picture.

"You must have loved her very much," I said.

For a moment Alex did not answer, and when he did his voice was short, "No," he said. "I didn't love her at all."

My understanding of Alex's feelings, that beautiful structure I had built up out of what he told me, came tumbling down. There was no longer any reason for his reticence, no longer any excuse for his harsh, abrupt words to me.

"But you said—"

He sighed. "We seem to be going around and around and getting nowhere. Why don't we leave it tonight? You're tired. It's been a rough day for you—a new place, new people, adjustments to make. We'll be better off to talk about this some other time. " He stood up and pulled me to my feet. "Myra will expect us back at the party," he said.

I felt as if I had been reprimanded by a teacher who found me a dense pupil. I held back, refusing to go where he would lead me. "You're treating me like a child," I protested, "telling me when to talk and when to keep silent. But I'm not a child. I'm the woman you're going to marry. I have a right to ask questions."

"Some other time. Come on, let's go back."

Suddenly, we were in a contest of wills. Alex was determined to take me back to the party; I was determined to stay until I had the answers I needed. He was between me and the light, his square, powerful frame towering over me, although I was not slight. If it had been a physical contest, there would have been no doubt as to the winner, but although he had hold of my hands, he was not exerting any real strength. I jerked my hands away from his and said, "No, Alex. I'm not going until you've told me everything."

"There's nothing else to tell."

"You haven't told me anything yet. You haven't made me see how it was—how you felt toward Elizabeth, the things you did together, how she died. Those are the things I want to know."

"You're asking me to spread out my life with Elizabeth to satisfy your curiosity? No, I won't do that. My God, what are you, some kind of ghoul?"

His contemptuous words hung in the air between

us, but I made no effort to answer them. So this was how it ended. This was why I had felt from the beginning that coming here foreshadowed tragedy for me. Because of course Alex didn't want to marry me now. And I couldn't marry him, knowing what he thought of me. Ghoul, he had called me. How could he understand so little? It wasn't macabre curiosity that made me want to know the details of Elizabeth's life and death. It was only that I wanted to understand. I could accept Alex's previous marriage if I understood. If Alex couldn't see that, he couldn't see anything.

At any rate, the contest was over, and he had won. I slackened my resistance and walked silently beside him back to the ballroom.

Britt appeared before us. "I want to dance with the bride," he said. As we walked toward the floor, he bent and said in a low voice close to my ear, "Quarreling already?"

I jerked back and looked at his face. The sudden gesture must have given me away, because he said, "I thought so. Alex isn't easy to get along with, and you're so much younger, you can't have much in common. I doubt if he deserves you."

We started dancing. It was a fast number, and talking was impossible. I felt relieved. I didn't want to discuss Alex with Britt. When we finished the dance, Britt said, "Whew! I've had my exercise for the night. I could use some punch. How about you?" Not waiting for an answer, he steered me toward the dining room.

"Do you want to talk about it?" he asked as we stood drinking our punch.

"About what?" I parried, pretending not to understand.

"The quarrel with Alex. You look all torn up inside. I'm a good listener, and I know how to keep my mouth shut." He finished his punch and put down the cup.

I was surprised at his perspicacity and was tempted to tell him about the quarrel and ask some of the questions bothering me. Alex and I were finished anyway; it couldn't hurt to talk to Britt. His handsome face was looking down at me with nothing but kind concern on its boyish planes. But somehow his eyes looked withdrawn and watchful, and it seemed as if he were a little too curious about something which, after all, was between Alex and me.

I said, "It wasn't important."

"Were you quarreling about his first marriage?"

He put his hands on the wall, one arm on either side of me and leaned forward, hemming me in. His bright blue eyes were looking down at me with an expression no woman can fail to recognize. Not an invitation, but the prelude to one. A look that said, If you're interested, we'll go on from here. If not, no hard feelings. I was surprised. I shouldn't have thought he would be disloyal to Alex. Yet perhaps he did not consider it disloyal after the quarrel. Perhaps he knew it was over between Alex and me.

I said, "I'd better go. Alex will be looking for me."

Britt dropped his hands and moved back. I hurried away.

Later, in my room, I thought of Alex's words.

"The master of Wisteria and his bride make a pact on their wedding night," he had said. "They promise to be faithful to eternity."

Had Alex and Elizabeth made such a pact? Was that the bond that tied him to her still?

The answer did not come. I could not believe that of Alex. With all his possessiveness, with all his fierce intensity which I only half understood, I could not believe him a party to the gruesome sealing of that promise.

I got into bed and lay stiffly, unable to relax my muscles or stop my thoughts. But gradually the grinding of my mind ceased; my thoughts began to drift, and finally I fell into a light doze. I was still aware of everything—the moonlight in the room, the loud ticking of the grandfather clock in the hall outside, the call of a bird in the garden. Suddenly I was aware of a different noise—the soft click of my doorknob as someone turned it. My eyes flew open.

A white figure floated across my room as slowly and silently as a cloud. But it was not a cloud. It was, or appeared to be, a woman. Her head was slightly bent, and shoulder-length black hair swung forward, so that all I saw was the black hair and a gauzy white garment which flowed to the floor. There was nothing frightful in what was visible of the apparition; yet it filled me with horror. I felt that the curtain of black hair in front of her face was hiding something ghastly, something that would not bear looking on.

I do not know what I should have done if she had turned toward the bed, but she did not. She seemed quite unaware of me as she drifted across the room and through the French doors.

It was a moment before my terror abated enough for me to move. Then I jumped out of bed and ran to the French doors through which she had disappeared. There was no sight of the white figure. Shivering with fear, I opened the doors and walked out on the sun deck. From here I could see the terrace below, the garden, even the swimming pool. There was no white figure anywhere. She had vanished into thin air.

I came back into the room, locking the French doors carefully and also the door to the hall. Shaking, I put on the robe which matched my yellow pajamas. I smoked seldom, but now, needing some activity to steady my nerves, I jerkily searched through my purse until I found a crumpled pack. The cigarette tasted stale and burned my throat; I stubbed it out.

Someone—or something—had come into my room, moved soundlessly across it, and disappeared through the French doors. I had not imagined it. I did not have nightmares or visions; sometimes I dreamed, but I was always aware of where reality ended and dreams began.

What if she came back?

My mouth went dry and my heart beat harder. I couldn't stay here alone with my fright. I started toward the door, but halfway across the room I stopped. Where was I going? To whom could I turn? I could imagine Alex's contempt; he would think my ghost more evidence of ghoulish curiosity. Myra would smile and soothe me as if I were a foolish child. There was Pam; she had seemed sympathetic. But I had already learned that she saw everything through Myra's eyes. Besides, it wasn't fair to disturb Chris, whose sleep must be frequently interrupted by medical emergencies. Remembering the way Britt had looked at me, I knew what meaning he would read into an appeal for help in the middle of the night.

There was no one I could go to for help.

Still, the ghost had not tried to harm me, indeed had not seemed aware of my presence. I was in no danger. Gradually my fear dissipated, my trembling stopped, and the blood came back into my hands and feet, warming them. I went back to bed. I did not expect to sleep, but I did.

Chapter 4

I woke unrefreshed, more tired than when I went to bed. Glancing at my watch, I saw that it was eight o'clock, and I was surprised that I hadn't slept longer after the sleepless hours last night. A knock sounded on my door, and I realized that I had heard it before, on the edge of sleep. It was that which had awaken me.

"Who is it?" I called.

"Me, Alex. Would like to go horseback riding before breakfast?" His voice sounded brisk and cheerful with no reminder of last night's quarrel. It was not what I expected—but then I hardly knew what I did expect. Once again I realized how little I knew Alex.

"I'll meet you downstairs in fifteen minutes," I

called, already getting into western style denims and a plaid shirt. I was glad he had awakened me. It would be easier to face him alone than in the presence of his family.

"That was quick," he said as I walked onto the terrace. "You look lovely. But a little tired. Did you sleep well?"

I hesitated, and before I could decide how to answer, he said, "We'd better get started. We'll have to make our own breakfast when we get back. Mrs. Gilbert has the day off, so everyone has to work on Sunday."

I said, "I can scramble eggs and make coffee, but that's about as far as my culinary talents extend, I'm afraid."

We went down the stone walk to the swimming pool. The walk was old; the stones were worn smooth by the uncounted footsteps of generations. But the pool was new. The concrete paving around it gleamed whitely, and there were as yet no plantings except a row of tall arborvitae bushes near the bathhouse. The blue-green water sparkled in the sun.

We turned left in front of the arborvitae bushes. "These look as if they've been here a long time," I said.

"Yes, they were planted by the storm cellar that is now under the bathhouse."

"Storm cellar?"

"An underground room to go into when a tornado strikes."

"Do you get many tornadoes?"

"There have been some bad ones in the area.

Wisteria has never been hit, but about five years ago several houses in Abbeville were destroyed."

At the mention of yet another danger here I shivered. He took my hand. "Are you afraid of storms?"

At his touch my heart beat faster. He was acting as if nothing had happened last night, as if everything was as it had been before we came here. I caught my breath and said, "No, I'm not afraid of storms, but then I've never been in one."

"I hope you never will be. But the storm cellar is there, just in case. Most people around here have them, and some go in every time a little cloud comes up. I haven't been in ours in years. We use it for storage space, and the water heater for the bathhouse is there."

The storm cellar is there just in case, he said. That must mean he expected me to stay at Wisteria. Perhaps it was his way of telling me the quarrel was unimportant.

We entered a patch of woods different from the dark tangled jungle we had driven through yesterday. This was a pine forest with little undergrowth. A clean fragrance scented the air, and splintered sunshine sifted through the needles. When we came out on the other side, I could see the white stables. A new pickup truck was parked at the side. As we neared it, I saw on the door a wisteria bloom and the words *Wisteria Plantation*.

A black man came out the door at the end of the building and stopped, looking toward us. Tall and slim, he wore glasses and had a neat mustache. I thought I had never seen such a *clean*-looking man in my life; everything about him seemed to shine—his glasses, his crisp blue work clothes, even his light brown skin. He took a few steps forward as we came closer and stood waiting for us with his hands in his pockets.

"Tracy, this is Jim Cantwell, my partner," Alex said. "Jim, Tracy Meadows. Something wrong, Jim?"

He spoke in a soft precise voice. "No, I meant to give Dawn a workout," he said. "Britt has been riding almost every day, but Miss Parker has her own horse, so Dawn hasn't had much exercise. Since you're here, I won't have to bother. You'll like Dawn, Miss Meadows. She's a beauty and needs just a light touch to guide her."

"I don't want you to change your plans for me," I said.

"Oh, Jim doesn't mind," Alex said. "He was only looking after Dawn the way he looks after everything on this place."

They launched into a discussion of business, and I looked around. The stables were as well kept as everything else here at Wisteria. Alex had said the farm was prosperous. I wondered what kind of partnership he and Jim had. He hadn't mentioned a partner before.

They finished their discussion, and Jim said, "I'll be going now. I'm glad to have met you, Miss Meadows."

"Call me Tracy," I said.

He looked surprised and glanced toward Alex. Then he looked back at me. "I really am glad to meet you. If there is anything I can do toward helping with the wedding, let me know. You'll be making some changes in the house, I expect, one of these days. I'll be glad to move furniture or do anything I can."

He sounded very earnest, and I thought, Why, he really is glad I've come. So far no one else had been, except Pam.

"I probably won't change the house," I said, "but I'm going to restore the garden, and I'll needs lots of advice from everyone. I love flowers, but I know very little about gardening."

"You've hit on something dear to Jim's heart," Alex said. "He's been wanting to see that garden cleaned out."

Jim said, "I've done a little pruning from time to time, but it needs a lot more than that. It was once a formal garden, clipped and disciplined, but it's gone to jungle now. What did you have in mind—formal or natural?"

"I rather thought formal, but I haven't seen it yet."

His eyes were bright. "Yes, I like that. There aren't many formal gardens in this area. It would be a showplace if you could get it done well."

Alex laughed. "Whoa!" he said. "You two can talk about the garden another time. I want to go riding."

Jim laughed too and said, "I was just leaving." He turned to me. "Let me know when you want to start the garden."

Alex and I walked toward the harness room. "Jim likes you," he said.

"I hope so. I liked him. But you didn't tell me you had a partner."

"I furnished the land and bought the equipment. Jim furnishes the know-how—he went to an agricultural college—and the labor. He and his two teen-aged boys do a lot of the work themselves. It's a good arrangement."

"Does he live close by?"

"About a mile down the road toward Abbeville. The land his house is on used to be a part of the plantation—his father was a tenant farmer for my father—but I sold him five acres soon after we went into partnership. It's only about a quarter of a mile to his place through the fields."

"You've known him a long time then."

"Lord, yes. We played together as boys. But look, Tracy, don't say anything about Jim's being a partner to anyone outside the family. Most people around here think he works for me, and that suits us just as well."

Naturally they would think Jim worked for Alex since it was Alex's farm. But I wondered why he said it suited them.

By then the horses were saddled. Dawn was a filly, sleek and golden, and, as Jim had said, a dream to handle. Toffy was a chestnut stallion, a bit skittish and with a wild look in his eyes. Alex seemed to manage him without difficulty.

I wondered about his name. "Toffee, as in candy?" I asked. It seemed an odd name choice. He wasn't the color of toffee, and he certainly didn't look sweet.

50

"No, Toffy for Mephistopheles," he answered. "He's a devil sometimes."

We rode through the strip of pine woods farther down the path, came out into a meadow that was a frothy sea of pink wildflowers, and crossed it to an old roadbed.

We turned the horses off the road and climbed the grassy slope. At the top, hidden from the road by a wild plum thicket, was a small cemetery of not more than a dozen graves surrounded by a rusty iron fence. We dismounted, and Alex opened the squeaky gate.

"There's no grass," I said in surprise. The entire enclosure had been carefully scraped clean; it was a square of sun-baked earth neatly fenced from the wild growth around it.

"When these people were buried, it was a disgrace to let a graveyard get grassy. So I keep it the way it has always been kept. I think they would want it that way."

"They would probably haunt you if you didn't," I said lightly. "*Do* they ever haunt you? Wisteria is such an old house; it must have a ghost or two."

He looked at me with an odd expression in his dark eyes, as if he were trying to read something behind my words. For a moment I thought he had caught my serious intent, and I was sorry I had spoken. I had made up my mind to say nothing of seeing the ghost last night, to say nothing at all that might bring up the subject of our quarrel. If Alex could forget it, so could I.

When he spoke, his words were as casual as

mine. "No, that's one thing you don't have to worry about. There are no ghosts at Wisteria."

We wandered around for a while reading the barely legible inscriptions on the age-darkened marble tombstones.

Alexander Rufus Farrington, 1806-1881. Rest in peace.

Martha King Farrington, 1816-1850. Beloved mother.

"Why, she was only thirty-four years old," I said.

"She died in childbirth. The baby is buried on the other side of her."

I went on reading the inscriptions. "Alexander never married again," I said. "At least, there doesn't seem to be another wife buried here."

"No, he had only one." He turned away from me.

"We should go if you want any breakfast. It will soon be time to get ready for church."

When we got back to the road, he said, "I'll race you back." I thought it would be no contest. The spirited stallion would win easily. However, I gave Dawn her head, and she surprised me. We got beaten but just barely. Alex helped me dismount, wiped the fine beading of sweat from my forehead, and held me wordlessly for a long moment. If I had been more sure of myself and of Alex, I wouldn't have wondered what that embrace meant. It could be a silent good-bye, a bittersweet regret that everything had turned out so badly. Or it might be, as I hoped, an apology for his harsh words last night, a way of saying I love you.

With a sudden shock I realized he had never said those words! Never. I had supplied them in my imagination, but he had not said them. He had said others: "I feel very possessive about you." "I've waited half a lifetime for you." I had thought they meant the same thing, but now I saw they didn't, not exactly.

I would ask him. I would say Alex, do you love me? Then however he answered, I would *know*. If he said yes, nothing could drive me away from Wisteria, not Myra's subtle insults, or the visitations of the ghost, or even Alex's strange behavior.

But Toffy gave a restless movement, and Alex said, "We must get these horses rubbed down." So I didn't ask the question after all. Perhaps later, while we were cooking breakfast, another opportunity would come.

When we got back to the house Myra was bringing a platter of scrambled eggs to a round table on the terrace. The table was set for six. I was disappointed. I had been looking forward to having Alex to myself a little while longer.

"Did you have a nice ride?" Myra asked cheerfully.

"Wonderful," I answered.

Myra was wearing a crisp blue-flowered housecoat, and beside her I felt suddenly hot and sweaty and knew the odor of horses clung to my clothes. Her nose wrinkled fastidiously.

Britt and Chris and Pam all came in at once. Britt's eyes flew to my face immediately. I thought he wanted to know if Alex and I had made up after our quarrel. He looked faintly dissatisfied with whatever he saw on my face. He turned to Alex and began talking about the horses.

Pam said to me, "How did you like Dawn?"

"She's a beauty. Alex and I raced back, and she almost beat Toffy."

"Yes, she has a lot of power for all her gentle ways."

"Do you ride much?"

"Now and then. Myra doesn't care for it," she said, as if that explained everything.

Chris looked up. "Golf is my game, but no one around here seems interested in it. There isn't a course within thirty miles."

"I thought you were from Abbeville."

"No, I'm from Memphis. Pam and I married before I got out of Med School. Then after I finished my internship, I came here to practice. The town needed a doctor, and I knew Pam would enjoy being close to her family." He smiled wryly. "I didn't mean to live here at Wisteria so long though."

Pam flushed and said, "I'm sure we'll find something soon."

Britt and Alex had stopped talking, perhaps caught by the same tension I felt. I thought this must be an old issue between Pam and Chris. Their attitudes seemed to say they had quarreled about it before.

"I heard yesterday that the Evans house is for sale," Britt said.

Myra answered, "Paul Evans' house on the Center Point Road? That house must be about twenty years old. It probably needs all kinds of repairs, and when you got through, what would you have? Bastard Tudor."

"No, not that one. The Evans house in town, Paul's father's house. Since the old couple died, it's been rented, but Paul told me he was going to sell it. He thought Pam and Chris might be interested."

"It isn't exactly what I've been looking for," Pam said slowly.

"You're looking for another Wisteria, and there isn't one," Chris said.

Britt glanced at him and looked back at Pam. "At least the Evans house is old," he said. "I've been inside it, and I remember the high ceilings and the carved mantel with an inset mirror."

Suddenly I saw something I hadn't noticed before. Britt wanted Pam to move from Wisteria. I wondered why.

"The house probably won't do, but I should at least look at it," Pam said.

"I wonder what the price is," Myra mused. "Too much, if I know Paul Evans. At any rate, you can't decide until you've seen it." She rose briskly, glancing at her watch. "It's forty minutes till church time. You'll have to hurry." She was already loading the dishes on a serving cart.

"Can I help?" I asked.

"No, I'm all ready except for putting on my dress. I'll load the dishes in the dishwasher and still have time left."

Sure enough, when we came down she was waiting for us, looking fragile and helpless in a soft blue knit dress. She looked sharply at each of the family, giving short nods of approval. Then she turned to me. She frowned. I fingered my pearls nervously, wondering what she could possibly find wrong with my pale yellow outfit. She said in a voice that sounded as if it meant to be comforting, "Riding always disarranges one's hair. Let me push it back a little. There now, I don't think anyone will notice."

"Too-perfect hairdos are a bit unfashionable now," I said, pushing my hair back the way it was before and looking pointedly at Myra's hair, which was stiffly sprayed to hold the flip at the ends. I was immediately ashamed of myself. I wouldn't descend to Myra's level; I wouldn't answer her again when she made those disparaging remarks. I would ignore Myra. All the same, I felt a little self-conscious about my hair.

Later, in my room, where I had gone to take a nap, I heard a knock at my door, and Myra came in. "I hoped I would find you still awake," she said. "Sandra just told me that she is going out of town for a few days, and I thought if you wanted her for a bridesmaid, we should tell her now. I don't know when you plan to have the wedding, but I rather gathered you are in a hurry."

I flushed, wondering if she meant to be nasty. Embarrassment made my words stumble. "There's no reason—I mean, I don't have to hurry—Alex wanted it to be soon, so I told Grandfather to come Friday, thinking we would get married Saturday or Sunday. But I could change that; Grandfather is flexible."

"I'm glad your plans weren't definite. I really

think it would be better not to rush. Getting married is a harrowing business at best."

"If we had a simple ceremony—"

"I thought you realized that wouldn't be suitable. A big wedding will take a little more time to arrange, but you'll be glad you took the time. Marry in haste and repent at leisure, you know."

My voice didn't stumble at all as I said, "You're making all these elaborate plans to delay the wedding, aren't you? That's what you've been after all along. Why?"

She sat down on the edge of my bed. "You don't know Alex very well. There are things—"

"You mean the mark of the Farringtons? I asked Alex about that. How could you think such a ridiculous story has anything to do with us?"

"Oh, my dear, I don't think. I know. Because of Elizabeth's scar."

While I stared at her with shocked eyes, she got up and said briskly, "I'll tell Sandra you want her for a bridesmaid." The door clicked softly behind her.

Chapter 5

We had supper on the terrace—chicken salad, cream cheese-and-cucumber sandwiches, and angel food cake with homemade ice cream.

"I don't see how you did this so quickly," I said to Myra. She had disappeared toward the kitchen not more than thirty minutes before.

"You should see Myra at work," Pam said. "She never gets hurried or flurried. She merely makes a few slow, easy movements, and there it is, all finished."

Myra looked pleased. "The secret is planning ahead. I've learned to be efficient. Heaven knows, if I hadn't, I would never have been able to keep this house and bring up two children."

"Where is Britt?" Alex asked, looking around.

"Here," Britt said, coming out the hall door. "I'm not going to eat though. I'm taking Sandra to dinner and a movie. Can you let me have a twenty, Alex? I'm a little short."

Alex handed him a bill. "It's a loan," he said pointedly.

I thought there was a flash of resentment in Britt's eyes, but he covered it by sticking out his chest and saying pompously, "Your money is secure with Abbeville's most promising young businessman."

He left, and Pam said, "Britt uses you, Alex."

"I haven't minded helping him," Alex said, "but I told him yesterday that he's on his own. He doesn't really need my help any longer, and now that I'm getting married—"

Myra said, "That reminds me, Tracy, it's all arranged for Sandra to be a bridesmaid. Pam can be matron of honor, but you'll need three more bridesmaids. I suppose you can get girls you knew in school? It might be a good idea to get in touch with them soon. The first of June is only three weeks away."

"The first of June? But we haven't set any date yet."

Myra raised her eyebrows. "Changing your mind again? Well, I suppose that's a bride's privilege. But I thought we had it all settled upstairs."

I didn't want to wait three weeks to marry Alex. I had a superstitious fear that if I waited, something might happen to prevent our marrying at all.

"Alex and I need to talk it over and decide on a date," I said now. I would tell Alex what I wanted, how I felt, and he could tell Myra. She would accept it from him, I was sure. I had already noticed that she didn't try to manage Alex as she did the others.

But to my astonishment he said to Myra. "I guess it takes time to arrange a big wedding. June first is fine with me."

"Then it's all settled," Myra said. She was serving the salad and didn't look up, but I had a feeling there was triumph in her eyes. Tears of anger and frustration sprang to mine.

After we had finished eating, Myra put Pam and me to work clearing away the supper and loading the dishwasher. When we got through, she had set up the Scrabble set on the library table. We played until eleven. By that time I was stifling yawns; I hadn't been able to take a nap this afternoon after Myra's dark hints about the mark of the Farrington's, so I'd had only about five hours sleep in two days.

I fell into bed and drifted off immediately, but I suppose I was too tired physically and emotionally to sink deeply into oblivion. My tightly strung nerves would not release me; my muscles twitched, and I turned restlessly. I was dreaming of running through a tangled thicket of wisteria. The vines reached for me, clutching at arms, legs, clothing. My heart beat fearfully; I was terrified of being caught by those grasping branches. Yet the harder I ran, the less progress I made. The shoulder-high bushes seemed to stretch for miles. I thought I would never get out.

Then with the abruptness that never seems

strange in a dream, the scene changed. I stood before a bearded, black-robed figure—seemingly a judge—who said in a solemn, reverberating voice, "Do you promise?" He turned his back, worked with something on a table behind him, and said again, "Do you promise?" Then I noticed that it was not a table behind him but some sort of brazier filled with glowing red coals. I saw that his gloved hands held a branding iron. The metal snapped and popped in the heat, and—

Suddenly I woke up, my heart still pounding with terror. I realized immediately that the hellish scene was only a dream, but its dreadful images were burned into my brain, and my eyes darted fearfully around the silent moonlit room.

I was not even surprised to see the ghost; it seemed merely an extension of the diabolical scene of my dream. It floated across the room as before and went through the French doors. This time my reactions were quicker. I jumped out of bed, not even taking time to grab my robe, and ran toward the French doors. I snatched them open just in time to see the ghost descending the steps to the terrace. Like a flash I went after it. It glided across the terrace, moving very fast. Running, I would have said, if anything so smooth and silent could be called running. I was right behind and steadily gaining ground. Even so, it reached the swimming pool area while I was still fifty or seventy-five feet away.

The moon went behind a cloud, and its silver radiance dulled to pewter, but there was still enough light to see the white figure dimly before me. It swerved and left the pavement for the lawn between the pool and the garden. Then it disappeared. Not suddenly, but in slow motion, like the melting of a candle. The slender figure about the height of an average-size woman sank slowly earthward, growing shorter and shorter until there was nothing left but a small blob of white on on the ground.

Filled with horror, I whirled and ran back toward the house, tore up the outside stairs and through my room, stopping only when I got to Alex's door. I pounded on it. Suddenly it jerked open. One look at my face and he cried, "What's wrong?"

For a moment I couldn't speak. Then I caught my breath and said, "Come quickly. There's something outside."

"What is it?" he asked as we hurried down the steps. But I didn't answer. I didn't know how to answer. He would see it; we would examine it together. Whatever the blob of white was, it wouldn't be so horrible if Alex were with me.

But when we got to the spot, I could see nothing at all—no ghost, no white spot on the ground, nothing. I stopped still, looking about. The garden was a dark tangle; anything could hide in there. But the open lawn, where the ghost disappeared, was empty. I walked slowly forward, keeping my eyes on the grass, and stopped where I thought the whit blob had been. The dew-wet grass seemed undisturbed. I could see no sigh of anything.

"What are you looking for?" Alex asked. "What frightened you?"

63

"I thought I saw someone out here."

His voice was rough and unbelieving. "This part of the yard isn't visible from your room. Now tell me what really happened." He shook my arm urgently.

I hesitated. I didn't think he would believe me. He said this morning there were no ghosts at Wisteria. So I told him the truth, but not the whole truth. "I woke up and went out on the sun deck, and I thought I saw someone in light-colored clothes moving around down here. I'm sorry I woke you for nothing, but I was frightened."

We turned and started toward the house. A few drops of rain spattered down, and Alex lengthened his steps so that I had to trot to keep up with him. When we got back to the terrace, he said, "Go up and get a warm robe and then come to my office. I want to talk with you."

When I got there, he handed me a glass. "Drink this."

I wrinkled my nose. "What is it?"

"Brandy. It's good for sudden crises."

I sat down on the brown leather sofa and pulled the robe together over my knees. Alex watched me with bright dark eyes as I drank the brandy. "You were shaking out there," he said.

"Was I? I didn't notice. At any rate, I feel fine now. The brandy does help."

"You were frightened half to death. I want to know all about whatever caused that fright."

I looked down at the tan carpet. It was woven in a swirling design. One could get dizzy if he looked at it too long. I said, "I've told you all I can. I saw something. I thought it was a—a person."

"Seeing someone on the lawn is hardly enough to throw you into the panic you were in when you knocked on my door. Didn't it occur to you that it could be one of us? Britt coming home. Or me. I sometimes take a walk at night if I can't sleep."

I looked at him and then away again. The picture on the opposite wall was an autumn scene; its yellows and oranges picked up the colors in the room. I gazed at it a long time, feeling his puzzled eyes on me. Finally I said, "All right, I didn't tell you everything. I don't know that I want to."

"Why not? Why are you so antagonistic all of a sudden? Have I done something?"

"No, it's just—" But I couldn't explain the forces that seemed to push us apart. I didn't understand them myself. "I didn't want to tell you because I thought you wouldn't believe me," I said rapidly. "And I was afraid you would be angry."

"Why should I be angry with you because you got frightened? I'm not that unreasonable, I hope."

"I thought it was Elizabeth who frightened me."

The blood drained from his face, and his eyes blazed at me. I said hopelessly, "There, you see, you are angry."

He swallowed and said, "No. No, I'm not. But I don't understand what you mean. Are you afraid my memories of Elizabeth will come between us? You don't have to worry about that."

"No, I mean Elizabeth herself. Or rather her ghost."

His eyes had not left my face. "That's rather a horrible joke."

"I knew you wouldn't believe me. But it's true. I did see it. The first time I thought I was dreaming, but then tonight . . ." My voice trailed off. "What's the use?"

"Go ahead and tell me. I want to hear it."

I told him all about the ghost. "I don't know what to think, Alex. You say there are no ghosts at Wisteria. But I saw one, and I'm frightened."

He sat down beside me and put his arm around my shoulder. "There has to be some explanation," he said slowly. "You were waked out of sleep both times. Perhaps you were not as awake as you thought. Couldn't the 'ghost' have been a retained image from your dream?"

"An image I followed all the way to the garden? No, I was awake, and I saw something."

"Then it must have been an optical illusion, a trick of the moonlight. Moonlight can give odd shapes to familiar objects. When I was a boy walking alone at night, I used to see a bear in every bush."

I was silent. He said, "I see you don't believe that either. But, Tracy, there are no ghosts, certainly not at Wisteria. In all the years, no one has ever seen one. If there had been a restless spirit here, it would have been seen before now."

We stared at each other.

"Why did you think it was Elizabeth's ghost?" he asked last. "Many people have died here. Why did you assume it was Elizabeth rather than someone else?"

I considered. "The size I suppose. It was a woman, not a man or a child. And the black hair. The portraits of the other Wisteria women all have blond hair like Pam and Britt."

He looked startled. "But Britt isn't—well, never mind. Elizabeth had black hair. Anything else?"

I hesitated. "This isn't objective, and you'll think it's my imagination. I *felt* that it was Elizabeth and that she wanted me to know it. You spoke of restless spirits. But that wasn't what I felt. It didn't occur to me that she was merely wandering about. I thought she had purposely come to my room, that I was meant to see her." I shrugged helplessly. "I don't know why I thought so. She didn't even turn toward me. But that was the feeling I had."

He was silent a long time. Finally he said, "I can't believe in ghosts, Tracy. What you saw in your room must have been a dream or the aftermath of one. Then when you went on the sun deck and saw someone below, you connected the two. It may have been one of the family; I'll ask tomorrow. If it was a prowler, I'll have to get a watchdog.

"It's only natural that you should be nervous and upset. Brides always are, aren't they? Bridegrooms, too, for that matter. You think of all the things that could go wrong and wonder if you are doing the right thing. But we are, Tracy; I'm sure we are. Trust me, honey."

Of course I trusted him. Whatever the evil forces were here at Wisteria, Alex had nothing to do with them.

The door opened, and Myra said, "Oh, pardon me. I didn't mean to interrupt anything. I heard voices and wondered if someone was sick. Is anything wrong?"

Her eyes widened as they moved from my yellow-robed figure to Alex in a navy robe and slippers. Her surprise seemed exaggerated, theatrical. I wanted to say, Don't pretend to be shocked. You know darn well nothing is going on down here. We're as covered up as we would be in daytime clothes. But I said nothing.

Alex moved his arm from around my shoulders. "Nothing is wrong. Tracy thought she saw a prowler, but we've decided she must have been mistaken. You didn't take a walk in the back yard a little while ago, did you?"

"Heavens, no. You know I never go out alone at night. I was asleep until I heard your voices."

She stood there a moment, but neither of us said anything more. I noticed that although she was wearing a pink peignoir, her blond hair was perfectly arranged, and she had on makeup. I wondered if she had carefully made up her face before coming downstairs. She said, "Good night then."

"Good night," Alex and I said together.

We lingered a few moments after she left, but our mood was broken, and soon we went to our rooms.

Chapter 6

I slept a little late and woke up feeling wonderful. Last night's clouds had gone without bringing rain; the sun was shining in a blue enameled sky. A mockingbird sang in an oak tree outside my window, and downstairs a vacuum cleaner hummed. I flung up a window. The fragrance of dew-laden wisteria came to me overlaid with the smell of frying bacon. In the brightness of the morning the problem of the ghost and the events of the night seemed far away. It was a day for doing things. Suddenly I thought, I'll buy my wedding dress today. I would not meekly accept Myra's plans. I would make all the preparations, and then we would see.

I slipped into a tailored jade green dress and

reached for my favorite piece of jewelry, my grandmother's cameo, which this year I wore pinned to a black velvet ribbon around my throat. My fingers hesitated and then moved frantically. The cameo was gone; the compartment in the little silver box was empty. Nevertheless, I went on looking for it, my fingers scrabbling in the box, unwilling to admit it was not there.

I hurried downstairs. Alex's office door was open, and he was sitting at his desk writing. He looked up as I went in. "Good morning, Tracy. Did you sleep the rest of the—" He broke off and said, "You look upset."

"Alex, my cameo is missing."

"The one you were wearing Saturday night? Where did you put it when you pulled it off?"

"In the little silver box where I always keep it. The box is on the dressing table in my room, but the cameo is gone."

"Perhaps you lost it at the party. We were on the terrace for a while. Have you looked there?"

"No, but I know I put it back in the box. I saw it when I dressed for church yesterday."

He moved impatiently. "It must be around somewhere. Get Myra to help you hunt it."

"There's no use to hunt. It was in the case yesterday, and I haven't worn it since."

"Look, Tracy, I've got an awful lot of work here after taking off last week. Can't this wait?"

"I suppose so," I said slowly. "Only it seems that the sooner we tell the police the better chance they'll have to get it back."

"Tell the police? Why should we do that?"

"When something is stolen, don't you have to tell the police? Otherwise you are concealing a crime, I think."

"But why would anyone steal your cameo? It's pretty enough, I don't mean that. But it didn't cost much, did it? I ordered some for the stores a couple of months back; I think they retailed for $2.98. You probably paid considerably more for yours in a jewelry store, but still—"

"It belonged to my grandmother."

"Oh, I see. It has sentimental value. I'll call Myra to help you hunt it."

I said desperately, "Alex, please listen. There's no use looking. It was in the box, and it's gone. We'll have to call the police."

He looked annoyed. "I'm willing to help you look for it, Tracy. We'll all help. But I don't know why you keep wanting to call the police. It's valuable to you, but sentimental value doesn't mean anything to them. They'll think you're making a big fuss over nothing."

"Is that what you think, too?" I asked slowly. "Because it doesn't seem nothing to me. I should think you would be concerned over a theft in your house, even if it were something without value."

"Of course." He ran his hand over his forehead, as if trying to brush away an irritation. "But there's no way it could have been stolen. There has been no one here except us. Of course Mrs. Gilbert and her daughters came in this morning, but I would trust them with my life."

Sudden comprehension flashed into his eyes. "The ghost! So that was what it was, a thief." Sev-

71

eral expressions chased across his face, incredulity, anger, puzzlement. "But why would anyone disguise himself as a ghost merely to steal a cameo?" he asked. "It seems too elaborate a plot for a few dollars gain."

"I've been trying to tell you. The cameo *is* worth stealing, to anyone who could recognize its value. It's one of the carnelian cameos done in Italy in the early sixteenth century."

"Oh. I should have known, but I keep forgetting you're a rich girl." He stared at me with consternation. "Is it insured?"

"Yes, of course. But it isn't the money I care about. I want the cameo back. My grandmother died before I was born, and the cameo and the pearls are all I have from her. Grandfather gave them to me on my sixteenth birthday, and he likes to see me wear them. He'll be as upset as I am."

"I'm terribly sorry." He looked past me. "Oh, Myra," he called, "come here a minute, will you?"

She came into the room and started to speak to me but fell silent, looking from one of us to the other. She looked trim and efficient in a blue housedress with her shining blond hair coiled neatly on top of her head.

"Tracy's cameo is missing, Myra. Have you seen it?"

"Didn't you have it on at the party?" she asked, "pinned on a black ribbon around your neck? It looked very nice, I thought. But I haven't seen it since. Where did you have it last?"

We went through all the questions again. Like Alex, Myra seemed to think I had laid the cameo down and forgotten it. But finally I convinced her I hadn't. While I was talking, something else occurred to me. "Wait a minute," I said. "Why didn't the thief take the pearls, too? They were in the same box. Anyone who realized the value of the cameo would almost certainly know the pearls were real."

Myra looked surprised. "I didn't dream your jewelry was so valuable," she said. "Diamonds are the only gems I recognize. It seems to me that whoever took the cameo must be very knowledgeable about jewelry. Alex, do you suppose we have a professional jewel thief in Abbeville?"

"I'm wondering about that, too. Tracy thought she saw someone out back last night, you know. We had decided she was mistaken, but now I'm not sure."

I was glad he didn't tell Myra I had thought it was a ghost.

"Could Pam have borrowed the cameo, not knowing its value?" Alex asked.

Myra looked shocked, "Pam would never borrow anything without asking." She looked at me, and her blue eyes were cold, as if I rather than Alex had made the suggestion. "It's quite possible you've misplaced it in your room. Got it out to wear perhaps and then decided not to and put it down somewhere."

"I'm sure I didn't lose it," I said, but my voice wavered. Under Myra's accusing stare, I was suddenly afraid I had misplaced the cameo.

"I'll make a search of Tracy's room," Myra said, taking charge. "We might as well not tell the others until we've made sure it really is gone." Her voice sounded brisk and reassuring. With the problem in capable hands, it seemed to say, there was nothing to worry about. She started out of the room, and I followed her. "You don't have to come," she said. "Why don't you have breakfast while I search?"

"No, I'll help you."

I had the feeling that she didn't want me with her when she searched my room, and that made me determined to be there. Somehow I didn't like the idea of Myra's being free to go through my belongings.

"It doesn't seem to be there," she reported to Alex fifteen minutes later. "You'll have to tell everyone, I guess. Chris and Britt are already gone, but Pam is upstairs. I'll get her. And I'll send for Mrs. Gilbert. The girls were here earlier, but they've gone to school now. I'm afraid Mrs. Gilbert will be upset. I wish this hadn't happened."

Although I had been here two days, this was the first time I had seen Mrs. Gilbert, the cook. Her face was square and padded with fat along the jawbone, so it looked bottom-heavy. The rest of her was fat, too, but solidly attached to a big-boned frame; she was the type of woman who is often told she carries her weight well. There was a frown between her gray eyes, and when she spoke, her voice was truculent. She said, "I hope you don't think me or my girls had anything to do with this."

"Of course not," Alex said hastily. "I only wanted to ask whether there was any stranger around here Saturday."

"I didn't see one. But I was tired. I don't like things to come up missing. If they're not found, it leaves a question in people's minds, and the ones that work there usually get blamed."

"There's no question of that," Alex hurried to say. "I'm sure we'll find the cameo, but even if we don't, we would never think of suspecting you or the girls."

"Well, I should hope not. If I thought you had any idea that me or the girls did this, I'd be obliged to quit my job right now."

"Oh, no," Alex said again. "I told Tracy just a few minutes ago that I'd trust you with my life."

She seemed somewhat mollified and after a few more protestations of innocence, she left.

"I wish I hadn't told her," Alex said. "It's natural she would be upset. But there was no way around it."

Pam came in as Mrs. Gilbert left. I explained again, and Pam said, "You mean someone came in the house and stole it? But that's unbelievable. The doors were locked at dark, weren't they? How could anyone get in? Unless he had a key, and that's too frightening to think about."

So for a different reason she was as upset as Mrs. Gilbert. I didn't feel so calm myself. At Alex's insistence I ate a little breakfast, but it was like chewing Kleenex.

Sheriff Bridges came about the time I finished and went straight to Alex's office. I saw him through the dining room door, and my heart sank. He was too much the theatrical stereotype of a Southern sheriff, fat and sloppy in a khaki uniform.

75

I thought he would be slow and stupid, covering ineptness with a blustering toughness.

But when I faced him in the library, I changed my mind. Slow he might be, slow-moving and slow-talking, but far from stupid. Without saying much himself, he kept me talking until the last detail of the theft had been given, and I almost told him about the ghost before I caught myself.

After he talked with me, he asked to see Myra and Pam. I wandered out to the terrace.

Behind the tall bushes of the garden something rustled loudly, and through the branches I caught a flash of movement. I was suddenly cold. Someone was out there now. Then Jim Cantwell walked into view. I let out my breath. "You frightened me," I said as he came up to the terrace.

"Sorry. I've been thinking about the garden ever since we talked yesterday morning, and I couldn't wait to get over here and see if my ideas were practical." The sun glinted on his glasses, sending out little flashes of blue and gold, and his words seemed to sparkle, too, as he talked of pruning and fertilizing and planting.

We walked down a partially graveled walk between rows of tall shrubbery. Branches brushed at us from each side. Small, tough weeds grew in the sparse gravel. In the beds beside the walks iris thrust determined purple heads above the dead stalks of last fall's chrysanthemums. I saw a few scrawny zinnia plants; they were volunteers, I guessed, which came up year after year.

Jim pointed to the broken sun dial, lying where

the walks converged. It was in three pieces, left carelessly on the ground, as if no one cared any longer to mark the sunlit hours.

"I'll have to dig the dial out and turn it over," Jim said. "It may not be damaged. If not, we can have a new base made."

I sat down on one of the concrete benches. Jim stood in front of me watching my face. "It isn't as bad as it looks," he said. "You're depressed this morning. I shouldn't have pressed you to do this."

"No, it isn't that." I looked at his kind brown face. "You are right though. I am upset. A cameo handed down from my grandmother was stolen from my room. Somehow Alex seems to blame me for it."

"Perhaps he's only worried. Sometimes it's hard to interpret what someone else is feeling."

"Maybe. But it seems as if coming to Wisteria has ruined everything. Alex and I quarrel..."

"I suppose both of you are nervous about getting married, Alex especially. It's different for Alex."

"They had been married only a year, hadn't they?"

"Yes, and she was sick a lot during that year. She went to the hospital two or three times, I remember. Alex never told me what was wrong with her."

I was surprised. "It seems as if he would have, your being such good friends."

His eyes slid around sideways to my face. He checked whatever he had been about to say and

77

said instead, "I don't think he talked much about it to anyone."

So even then Alex had kept what he felt about Elizabeth to himself. I wondered what was wrong with her. No one had said she was an invalid.

"I suppose he took her death hard," I said.

He frowned and looked doubtful. "It's difficult to understand how Alex feels about anything," he said at last. "He keeps it inside. He worked harder than usual that year, I remember. Stayed at it night and day. 'Leave some for tomorrow,' I used to say, but he would look at me with stony eyes as if he thought tomorrow wouldn't come. And didn't care."

I was silent, hearing Alex saying "I didn't love her." Perhaps he only said that to keep peace with me. Some powerful emotion had held him—was still holding him—to Elizabeth, and what emotion is as strong as love?

After a pause Jim said, "Whatever Alex felt about his wife's death, he got over it. Or rather, he put Wisteria in the place of it. For years now he has given all his time and attention—and love—to this place. That's why I was so glad when he told me he was going to get married again. Love ought to have a human object; it isn't right to concentrate it on a pile of wood and brick and a spot of ground."

"Wisteria is a beautiful house," I said. "Alex has been telling me some of its history."

"There's plenty of that—some that even Alex doesn't know, I guess. I daresay the story he told you is different from the one I would tell."

"In what way?"

"A different viewpoint. Alex knows it from the side of the plantation owners; I know it from the side of the slaves."

"There was only one slaveowner here, wasn't there? Alexander Rufus Farrington, the first owner? Alex hinted that he was cruel."

"He used to brand his slaves like cattle."

I stared at him, speechless.

"I've heard my grandmother tell about it many times. She was born after the war, but she had the story from her mother. Yes, I would say cruel was a mild word for it."

I felt choked, unable to get my voice above a whisper, but I had to ask. "Did he also brand his wife?"

Jim looked at me sharply, "Who told you that?"

"Alex hinted at it."

"Oh. Well, I wouldn't be surprised if it's true. He liked possessing things and marking them for his own . . . I don't mean to sound bitter. Those days are gone, thank God. We live in a better world, and it's improving all the time. My father would turn over in his grave if he could hear me calling Alex by his first name. Alex's father would, too, I expect, even though he made me Alex's playmate and later sent me to college."

"Why shouldn't you call Alex by his first name? You've known each other all your lives."

"In the old days I would have switched to 'Mr. Alex' when we were about twelve years old. Calling him Alex is a small thing maybe, but it's a symbol of change. But don't get me started on race relations. It's a subject so complicated we could talk about it all day."

"I'm afraid I don't know much about it," I said apologetically. "I was brought up in a private school where we had only a few black pupils. I've never paid much attention to the color of a person's skin."

"I appreciate that. But I hope it won't cause any trouble for your down here."

"Why should it?"

He looked at me. "Maybe it won't," he said slowly. "You may be good for Abbeville in more ways than one."

"Jim, there's something else I'd like to ask you, if you won't mention it to anyone."

He nodded.

"Have you ever seen a ghost here at Wisteria?"

He looked offended. "Nawsuh, Miss Tracy, I'd be skeered to death of a ghost," he said in an exaggerated Negro dialect totally different from his usual cultured speech.

"Why are you talking like that? Did I say something wrong?"

He examined my face. "I'm sorry. I thought you were making fun of me. I should have known better. You're serious, aren't you? No, I've never seen a ghost. I don't believe in ghosts. Why?"

"Because one has been in my room both nights I've been here."

"Exactly what did you see?"

I told him, and he said slowly, "It wasn't a ghost, Tracy. A dream perhaps. Fear of the change you are making in your life, something like that."

It was the same thing Alex had said, and it satisfied me no better coming from Jim. But I said no more. We walked on through the garden, speaking only of the changes we might make. Then Jim said he would make a few diagrams before we talked again.

I returned to the house. Myra met me in the hall. "I was just starting to look for you," she said. "I thought we could go by to see Mrs. Johnson, the florist. We need to give her the date of the wedding and tell her what we'll want."

"If you don't mind, I would rather not this morning," I said. "One more day won't matter, will it?" I still didn't want to commit myself to the wedding date Myra had chosen.

"I suppose not." She hesitated. "Is something wrong? Some trouble perhaps between you and Alex?"

"No, of course not."

"I didn't mean to pry. I couldn't help noticing that he was irritated about your losing the cameo. I'm afraid Alex hasn't much patience with carelessness, especially with valuable objects. And of course having to call the law was embarrassing for him. The news that we've had a theft out here will be all over Abbeville by nightfall."

That consequence of my loss had not occurred to me. I went into the library. Perhaps reading should not be used for a drug, but it had helped me through some sad, lonely times, and I thought it might work now.

I was reading the titles, which ran largely to the Victorian classics, when Britt's voice intruded.

"Tracy, Pam tells me you've lost a valuable piece of jewelry."

"Not lost. It was stolen." I spoke more sharply than I intended, because I was still irritated by Myra's words about my carelessness. I said, "I'm sorry, Britt. I'm edgy this morning. Are you home for lunch already?"

"I'm early. Pam stopped by the store on her way to see Paul Evans about the house, and when she told me about your—theft—I came straight home."

"That was good of you, but there's really nothing you can do. I've already talked to Sheriff Bridges, and I'm sure he'll do everything possible."

He came in the room and sat down on the velvet sofa. "I'd like to help if I can."

Britt had offered to help before, the night of the party. I suspected him of having an ulterior motive then. I wondered if he had one now. He said, "I'm particularly concerned about this, because it isn't the first time it has happened."

"Not the first time? What do you mean?"

"Two years ago I was engaged to a girl named Lucy Wright. I had given her a ring, a two carat diamond solitaire. It was lost—or so she said— while she was visiting here."

"But I thought—that is, Pam said you and Sandra had been steadies since high school."

"Yes, except that few months I was infatuated with Lucy. It was infatuation, not love. But I didn't know that until I brought her home to introduce her to the family."

He paused, looked at something out the window

behind me, and then brought his eyes back to my face. "Lucy wasn't—I don't quite know the right word. Suitable—Myra would say. She was a flashy blond, overdressed and undereducated. I think she had gone to college to find a rich husband, and she thought I was it. But she didn't fit in here at all. We quarreled several times. The third day she was here she told me she had lost the ring. She said she left it on the basin in her bathroom, and when she went back it was gone."

"And you never found it?"

"We didn't look for it. You see, I didn't think she was telling the truth. I thought she had seen the end coming, as I did, and wanted to keep the ring. She was that kind."

"So you never knew what happened to it?"

"No. I wasn't happy at losing that much money, but what could I do? I thought of suing her to get it back, but I knew the family would never agree. So I told myself I was lucky to get out so cheaply and put it out of my mind. I didn't even mention it to the family; I was too embarrassed at being such a fool."

I said slowly, "Britt, do you think someone here is a thief?"

He frowned, looked embarrassed, and said, "I don't know, Tracy. It's an impossible thought, isn't it? Because it would have to be someone in the family or one of the Gilberts, and that's almost as bad."

"Forgive me, Britt, but there's Sandra. She has the run of the house. If she were jealous of you and Lucy—"

He shook his head decisively. "Sandra's too honest. Look Tracy, don't say anything about Lucy's ring, not yet anyway. After all, it's not likely to be found after two years. But all the same, your losing the cameo gives me hope it's still here, and I could use the money tied up in it. I'm going to turn the house upside down looking for it. And the cameo, too, of course."

I stared after Britt as he left. He was a puzzle to me. Since that one advance the night of the party —if anything so subtle could be called an advance— his manner toward me had been perfectly correct. Kind. Helpful. Yet underneath his helpfulness there always seemed to be an advantage for Britt.

Chapter 7

Pam was back for lunch, waving a house key. "You promised to help me house hunt, Tracy. Can you go this afternoon? The renters have moved out of the Evans house. It isn't cleaned up, but Mr. Evans said we could go ahead and look."

I didn't know how much help I would be to Pam, but I was glad to put my mind on her problems and rest from my own. "I'm hoping you'll change my luck," she said. "Myra and I have been looking for a house all year without finding anything suitable, and Chris is getting impatient. He wanted to start building months ago, but I thought we would get more for our money by buying an old place."

I nodded. "I should think there would be lots of older houses around here."

"Yes, but most of the good ones stay in the same families. I wasn't enthusiastic when Britt first mentioned this place, but after talking to him, my hopes have gone up."

"He did sound encouraging," I said. "You and Britt are very close, aren't you?"

"I doubt if anyone is very close to Britt. But I understand him pretty well, I think. He doesn't fool me as he does Alex and Myra. Maybe it's because we're kin and more alike than I realize."

"You don't seem much alike, except in looks. You must resemble your mother's people. Neither of you looks like Alex."

She looked at me in astonishment. "I thought you knew. Britt isn't any real kin to Alex. He's my half-brother. Daddy adopted him when he married Mother."

"Nobody mentioned that." But I realized that Alex had started to once.

"We hardly ever think of it. I mean, it's just the same as if Britt were born at Farrington. He was only two when he came to Wisteria, so he can't remember ever living anywhere else. And of course Daddy treated him like a real son."

We turned another curve, and a farm truck loomed in front of us. I shut my eyes, sure we were going to crash into it. When I opened them, the road in front was empty. I glanced back and saw the truck chugging along in the cloud of yellow dust we had raised. Pam had not stopped talking. I supposed the part I missed was about Britt and Sandra, because she said, "—but if Britt does marry her it will be when he sees some financial advantage to it."

"Perhaps he is afraid to trust anyone after Lucy," I suggested.

She threw me a sharp glance. "Did he tell you about that? I don't think it touched him very deeply. He broke the engagement himself. Lucy was completely unsuitable, and they didn't get along well. The weekend she spent at Wisteria the atmosphere was so tense I was uncomfortable every minute. Of course, Myra carried it off with her usual aplomb.

"Britt will do all right for himself, you can depend on that," Pam said. "He says his ambition is to be the richest man in the state. That reminds me—I hope you'll insist that Alex stick to his resolution not to lend Britt any more money. Alex is an easy mark for Britt."

"I hadn't thought of Alex's being an easy mark for anyone," I said slowly.

"Oh, he looks fierce, but he's as soft as jelly, and Britt takes advantage of that. He'll bleed Alex dry if he gets half a chance. I wouldn't say that to anyone else, but you're practically in the family already."

"So many things have gone wrong that I sometimes wonder if I ever will be in the family. Perhaps our marriage is not meant to be."

"Don't think like that. You're just nervous. Everyone goes through that period of doubt, I think. I know I did."

Pam slowed down. We bumped off the graveled road onto pavement. To the right, I saw a brick building surrounded by a cluster of small white houses. "The cotton mill and the mill village," Pam said. "The mill used to run night and day, but with the new synthetics and the competition from Hong Kong there is only one shift now. However, we have a sawmill and a new shoe factory."

We turned a curve, passed a service station with a rack of glass dishes out front, and suddenly we were on the main street of town. It was a two-block-long jumble of old red brick buildings with weathered wooden signs: Davis & Son, General Merchandise, Abeville Billiard Parlor, Miss Mary's Dress Shop, Claymore Variety Store, The Ritz Theater. Candy wrappers and empty cigarette packages littered the cracked sidewalks and at the end of the second block a deserted building was boarded up. Only a few people were on the street, and they moved slowly, as if they had nowhere to go.

"There's Britt's store," Pam said, gesturing toward a big parking lot backed by a group of modern buildings: a supermarket with price signs plastered over the glass front, a drug store proclaiming discount prices, and Roy's Top Value Store. Through the solid glass front I could see racks of bright-colored clothing.

We left the business section behind. Now the street was lined with huge water oaks, so old their roots had cracked and buckled the concrete sidewalk. Two-story frame houses sitting back from the street on green lawns looked solid and dignified.

Pam turned into a driveway toward the end of

88

the second block, and we got out. The house was tall and narrow with a porch running around two sides of it. It was painted medium gray, the color of dirty smoke, and the paint was peeling in great strips. The doorsteps looked uneven, and the screens were rusty.

Pam said, "It's ugly, isn't it? But painted a different color and with the gingerbread trim back on—I don't know."

Pam apparently saw beneath the surface of the grimy house. She exclaimed over the curving stairway, the elaborate archway between the living room and hall, and the dado in the dining room. She planned where she would put various nonexistent pieces of furniture. The broken-down sink and the one homemade wooden cabinet in the kitchen dampened her enthusiasm for a moment; then she said, "We'll have to rebuild this completely, but at least it's big enough to put in everything one could want. I don't care if I have to stack my dishes on a table until we can get it redone. I think this is it, Tracy. I can't wait for Myra to see it."

Two short toots of a car horn sounded in the driveway. "Why, it's Chris," Pam said.

We walked through the house again. Chris dismissed the griminess casually, "A good cleaning and a coat of paint will take care of that," he said. "What we need to be concerned with is the basic structure of the house." He raised and lowered a window, examined the baseboards, pulled back the broken linoleum and looked at the floor. "Everything fits tightly, and I don't see any sag. The foundations seem to be solid."

"You like it then?" Pam asked eagerly.

"Yes, I do. It seems worth the money, and I think you could have fun fixing it up."

"What about upkeep?" she asked hesitantly. "You won't complain later, will you?"

"We would have upkeep on any house. Once you get this fixed up the way you want it, I don't think upkeep will be a significant factor."

After what Pam had said about how careful Chris was with money, I wondered at the way he minimized the drawbacks. He must be even more anxious to move than I had realized.

Pam was delighted with his reaction. "I love it, but I didn't want to tell you until you looked at it." An anxious expression crossed her face. "Do you think Mr. Evans has any other prospective buyers?"

"I don't know. News gets around pretty fast, and I do know that Althea Jones and Bill Treadwell are looking for a place. They're getting married next month, you know."

"Chris, I'll just die if someone beats us to it."

"Shall I call him when I get back to the office and tell him we've decided?"

She turned suddenly cautious. "No, I don't want to make up my mind definitely quite yet. I'd like to have Myra see it first. She knows so much more than I do about remodeling and redecorating."

Chris flushed angrily and started to say something. Then he looked at me and fell silent.

"Could you tell him we're interested but haven't quite decided?" Pam asked.

"Yes, but he won't hold it for us if someone else

wants it. It wouldn't be fair to ask him to." He looked at her expectantly. For a moment I thought she would say yes, but after a pause she shook her head. "It's such a big step. I just can't make up my mind so suddenly. Besides, Myra's feelings will be hurt if I don't consult her."

He looked at her a moment longer. Then he said, "I'd better get back to the office."

Through the window she watched him get into the car. Her eyes were unhappy as she turned back to me. "He's disappointed that I couldn't decide," she said. "He thinks I'm too dependent on Myra. But we've always been close, and I can't turn my back on her just because I'm married."

"Myra seems the most successful stepmother I've ever met."

"I guess I bore people talking about how wonderful she is. But it's all true."

"Do you remember your real mother at all?" I asked.

"No," she said. Then her voice hardened. "It's just as well. She ran away with another man when I was only three years old, and we've never heard from her since. I guess I never really had a mother, because Myra always seemed more like a big sister. She has been wonderful," she said again.

Chapter 8

When we got back to Wisteria, Myra called to us from the living room. "We're having a swimming party at five o'clock. Spur of the moment, but I've called everyone, and there'll be a crowd. How did you like the house?" she added as an afterthought.

"I'm crazy about it," Pam said enthusiastically. "It's in bad shape now, but Chris says it is structurally sound. I wanted you to see it, but now with the party—"

Myra smiled indulgently. "There's no hurry about the house, is there? It will still be there tomorrow."

"Yes, but I don't want someone else to get ahead of us before we decide. Chris says Althea Jones and Bill Treadwell are looking for a house."

"I doubt if they'll be interested in that one. It was built back around the turn of the century and hasn't been modernized much. There will be an awful lot of expense to make it livable."

"But once it's done, it will be lovely," Pam said, her eyes full of dreams of lace curtains and velvet armchairs. "I know you'll like it as much as I do."

"Well, we'll see," Myra said. "You're like me, you like old things. But old isn't everything, you know. Sometimes those late Victorian houses can be pretty horrible."

For the first time I could see doubt in Pam's eyes. She was wondering whether the rococo woodwork, the arches and dados and the huge carved mantel, could be made a delightful part of the decor, or whether they would be too gaudy and pretentious. I saw her eyes go slowly around the living room, seeing the low ceilings, the clean white mantel, the graceful lines of Chippendale and Sheraton furniture, comparing all that with the ornateness of the other house. No, I wanted to cry, don't let Myra take your vision away. The other house isn't Wisteria, but it can be lovely in a different way.

I went up to my room and started a letter to Grandfather. He would arrive Friday, expecting the wedding to be Saturday or Sunday. Now Myra had changed the date. Yet I still wasn't sure I was going to accept her choice of June first. I hardly knew what to tell Grandfather. I started three times, but each time I wadded up the paper and threw it in the wastebasket. There seemed no way to tell him anything without letting my resentment creep into the letter.

Suddenly I realized that the house was too silent. As the clock struck five, the reason came to me. Everyone had gone to the pool. I jumped up and hurried into a swim suit. As I walked into the hall, I saw Britt coming out of Myra's room. He closed the door behind him very quietly. Then he saw me, and a look of startled dismay flashed over his face. It was gone in a moment. He smiled and said, "I'm caught. I've been searching Myra's room. Don't look so shocked. I told you I was going to search the house."

"Yes, but to do it secretly! I don't know; it seems dishonest somehow."

"Tracy, we have to be realistic. The thief could be anyone, even Myra. There's no use searching if I warn them ahead of time. It wasn't Myra though. I didn't find a thing. Wait a minute while I change, and I'll walk down with you. I want to hear about Pam's house."

I wondered again why he wanted Pam to move. He said, "They'll be better off in their own home. All of us will be better off."

I thought of Pam's insistence that Alex not lend Britt any more money. Perhaps she did understand him.

I remembered some of the people from the party Saturday night and recognized other names I had heard mentioned. I met Althea Jones and Bill Treadwell, the couple Chris said were looking for a house. They were in their late twenties, and I learned that they both taught in the local school.

No doubt their marriage would be a success; they knew each other's interests and backgrounds and what the pattern of their lives would be. I envied them.

By that time Alex and I were close to the table of food, and I said, "I'm hungry. Will it hurt to eat before I swim, or is that only an old superstition?"

"I don't think you could really call this eating," Alex said, eyeing the tiny sandwiches. "Go grab that empty chair, and I'll bring you something."

As I sat down, I recognized Myra's voice behind me. "It could be an attractive place with the right furnishings," she said. "Pam looked at it—she has looked at every house for sale in Abbeville the past year—but I don't think she'll want it. After all, they're quite comfortable here, and there's no reason for them to move."

"Thanks for telling me about it," a feminine voice answered. "Bill and I will see Mr. Evans in the morning."

Why, Myra was telling Althea about Pam's house! My face felt hot, and instinctively I scrunched lower in my chair. Any minute she'll see me, I thought, and realize I've overheard. But she moved away. About that time Alex came with drinks and a plate of food. While we ate, I told him about the house and how much Pam liked it. I didn't mention overhearing Myra tell Althea about it.

We slid off the edge into the deep end of the pool. The water was just right, cool enough to refresh without shocking. Alex stated his intention of getting some real exercise and struck off across the pool, but I turned on my back and swam slowly, looking up at the blue sky. Other swimmers were nearby, but I paid no attention to them, thankful that here at least I was not expected to smile and talk.

The sky overhead was turning from blue to gray with approaching darkness, but I kept sculling about, lost in my pleasant dreams. Suddenly I went under. I gasped at the shock and swallowed a mouthful of water. It took a moment to realize that something was holding one of my legs. Puzzled, I kicked vigorously, trying to shake free. What could be holding me? I began to be frightened. My throat ached, and my head felt tight. I kicked again harder, putting all my strength into the downward thrust. Nothing happened.

Then I knew it wasn't something holding me; it was somebody. I could feel the hands encircling my leg, pulling me down. I twisted my head, trying to look backward and see who it was. Alex, playing a joke? Anger flashed through me. This wasn't funny. This was deadly serious.

Alex would not be so foolhardy. It was someone else, playing a deadly trick.

With the falling darkness the water was no longer bright. In its murky depths I couldn't have recognized anyone, even if I could have faced him. Panic flooded my mind. I must not breathe; I must not. Alex, help me, I cried silently. But Alex did not come. I knew that soon it would be too late. All of life became one gigantic agonizing effort to keep my aching throat locked against the pressure in my lungs. My arms and legs were like lead; I couldn't kick anymore. I had no body, only two heavy bands of steel where my chest and throat should be. The bands would hold; they must hold. I would not breathe. The pressure increased, became unbearable. I gasped and felt the water go into my lungs. I fought against the terrifying pain, the dark enormous pain bigger than the world. The blackness grew deeper, engulfed me. I felt myself drifting away toward a bright meadow where the air was sweet and fresh and I could breathe deeply and easily. I was lying in the sweet-smelling grass resting. It was not necessary to move. I could lie here forever with the sunshine warming my shoulders and birds twittering nearby.

Something was disturbing my rest. I coughed and gagged. Gradually the dream faded. I realized that the warmth I had felt was the sun-heated concrete beneath me, and the twittering was not birds but excited voices.

"She's coming around," someone said.

With a tremendous effort I focused my eyes and saw Alex's face above me, dark and fierce. "Help me get her in the house," he said.

Chapter 9

I was downstairs early the next morning, but even so I found the rest of the family already at breakfast.

"We didn't expect you down so soon," Alex said, getting up to pull out my chair. "How do you feel?"

"Fine," I answered, surprised to find that it was so. Then I realized why. Knowing someone wanted to kill me added anger to my fright and stiffened my backbone.

"You really gave us a scare," Alex said. "Afterward you seemed to be hysterical. You kept trying to tell me that someone tried to drown you. Chris finally gave you a shot to calm you down and make you sleep."

"Someone did try to drown me," I said. "Someone caught hold of my ankle and pulled me underwater."

They were all staring at me with shocked faces. I looked from one to the other trying to find a face on which the shock was only simulated, but I could not pick out the face of guilt.

"That's incredible," Alex said. "Why would anyone want to drown you?"

"I don't know. To keep me from marrying you?"

His eyes flashed to Myra and then quickly looked away. But I had seen the look, and I wondered what it signified. Suspicion, perhaps. Or conspiracy.

No, Alex loved me.

"If you're going to suspect one of us, you might as well suspect us all," Britt said. "We were all swimming at that time. In fact, the pool was full of swimmers. I wonder why no one noticed your struggles."

"I didn't struggle until I got underwater; it happened too quickly. By the time I realized the danger and started struggling, it was so dark down there I doubt if anyone would have noticed unless he swam right up on us."

"Which is what I did," Alex said. "When I noticed you were missing, I dived under where I had seen you last. You were on the bottom of the pool. I didn't see anyone else."

A thought flashed into my mind. Was there no one there—or no one visible? Could a ghost swim? Perhaps I was wrong to think my danger was from a human source.

"Naturally Tracy doesn't remember clearly what happened," Myra said. "Almost drowning—that's a traumatic experience. It's enough to make her suspect everyone."

"Don't think about it any more," Pam advised. "None of us would try to drown you, and no one else knows you well enough."

"I think that turned out to be an oblique insult, Pam," Britt said.

Not much got by him.

Pam thought back and said, "I'm sorry, Tracy. You know I didn't mean it that way."

"Pam is right though," Britt said. "You must be mistaken. Perhaps you got a cramp or something."

"You had been eating just before we went in," Alex said, "I didn't think it would hurt, but maybe I was wrong."

I didn't reply. I knew it was no accident.

"Myra, can you go to see the house this morning?" Pam asked.

"I don't see how, Pam. I have several household chores to do, and then Tracy and I should start making some arrangements for the wedding. We need to see the minister and the florist."

"Don't worry about that," I said, "We can do it tomorrow. I want to go to the city today and select the dresses for the wedding. I need to do that before I decide on flowers."

"All right. What time do you want to leave? I can be ready in a few minutes."

"No, you and Pam go and look at the house. I can do the shopping alone."

101

"The house can wait," she said. "You'll need someone to help you make the selections. It's hard to decide on anything when you're alone."

I saw that she was quite determined to go with me, but I didn't want her along. I wanted to pick out my own wedding dress. Also, I intended to ask them to hurry with the dress, and I didn't care for Myra to know just yet that I was hoping to get married at the end of the week.

Britt had been sitting silently, apparently not listening. Yet I knew he had heard every word, because he said, "After you get through at the house, Myra, I'd like you to come by the store. I need your advice on a new line of women's dresses."

"Can't that wait until tomorrow, Britt? I really feel I should go with Tracy."

"No, I have to decide today."

She capitulated. "If you're sure you don't need me, Tracy—I'll give you Sandra's size, and Pam can tell you hers. They aren't hard to fit."

"Is there anyone in town who does alterations?" I asked.

"Yes, Mrs. Bailey is a good seamstress."

"Then it will be more convenient to have the bridesmaids' dresses done here, so the girls won't have to go back and forth."

It would also save time. I could bring everything back with me today except my dress, which I would pick up later. By the end of the week everything would be ready.

I went into the store when it opened at nine-thirty, and three hours later I came out with a load of boxes I could barely see over. Fortunately, I had parked Alex's car close by, and I was almost to it when I heard a familiar voice say, "Can I help you?"

A brown hand lifted off the top boxes. "Why, Jim, how nice," I said. "I didn't expect to see you here."

"I didn't expect to be here, but I had to make an emergency trip to the dentist."

"Nothing serious, I hope."

"It seems serious to me. But no, it isn't really."

"Can you eat? I'm going to lunch now, and there's something I want to tell you. I think I saw a restaurant in the next block."

"I can eat," he said slowly, "but I'm not sure we should eat together."

"Why not?" I asked in astonishment.

He gave me a level look. "Because you and I aren't the same color. It's one of the things that just isn't done in Abbeville."

I thought that over. I was going to live in Abbeville, and I didn't want to offend people. But I felt if I backed down now, it would be an unforgivable offense to Jim and to my self-respect. I would be saying Abbeville's opinion was more important than what I knew to be right. So I said, "I think that's a custom I'll ignore. So come on. Unless you would rather not?"

"No," he said, still in that slow, considering way. "No, I'll come."

The restaurant turned out to be a large cafeteria beautifully decorated and filled with well-dressed people. After we selected our food, white-coated black waiters took our trays and escorted us to a table. I wondered how Jim felt toward the waiters, and then I realized how ridiculous that was. I didn't have any special feeling about white waiters, did I? But I was suddenly conscious of skin color in a way I had never been before. I noticed other blacks in the restaurant, but they were in little groups. None of them were with white people.

When we were seated, I said, "You feel all right about this now, don't you?"

"No," he said frankly. "No, I don't. But I don't know whether I can make you understand why. I think segregation is wrong, but a lot of white people I've known and respected all my life don't, and I don't care to offend them."

"Isn't that cowardly?"

He was silent. Perhaps I had offended him. I looked down at my plate.

Jim said, "I suppose it is cowardly to try to keep their good will by following their customs when I don't believe in them." He picked up his fork, put it down again, and said, "I was the first black student at my college, and that wasn't easy. Alex's father sent me there, but he wouldn't have sat down at the same table with me."

"Then why did he send you to a white college?"

"Because he thought blacks had as much right to a good education as whites. And *his* father wouldn't have thought that. So you see, we've made some progress." He sighed. "I'm older than you are, Tracy. I'm willing to make some compromises—even willing to admit they may be wise ... At any rate, we aren't in Abbeville, so let's forget it and enjoy our meal."

"I will enjoy it," I said. "I don't think I've ever appreciated before how good it is simply to be alive. I guess we don't until something happens."

He looked startled. "What has happened?"

"Someone tried to drown me in the pool yesterday."

"Who?"

"I don't know." I told him how it happened. "It could have been anybody at the party," I finished. "But as Pam pointed out, no one at Abbeville knows me except the Farrington family. Jim, there's something strange, something unnatural, at Wisteria."

"There's nothing strange about evil. It happens everywhere."

"Yes, I suppose so. Oddly enough, I feel better now that this has happened. I mean, at least it seems a human evil." I shivered. "I'm frightened, of course, that whoever wants to kill me will try again. But at least he can't come through locked doors. I have some chance to protect myself."

"Tracy, the only way to protect yourself is to leave Wisteria."

"You mean not marry Alex?"

"Put your wedding off for a while. This all started after you came here to marry Alex, didn't it? So if you go away, it should stop."

"That would be only a temporary answer. No, I have a better idea, Jim. I want to have the wedding sooner instead of later. If the purpose is to keep us from getting married, then once it's done the danger should disappear."

"Setting the wedding date up may only make whoever it is get in a hurry."

"Even that—if he gets in a hurry he may make some mistakes. We may catch him."

"Tracy, it's too much risk. He might get caught, but you might be dead. Dead, Tracy."

I shivered. "No, I'm on my guard now. And anyway, I don't plan to tell anyone except Alex about the change of plans until the last minute. What I want to do is catch them by surprise, have the wedding over before anything can happen. A *fait accompli*."

"It might work. But I'm worried. I wouldn't want anything to happen to you."

I had a little more shopping to do after lunch, so I didn't get back to Wisteria until five. Alex must have been watching for me, because he came out his office door just as I stopped the car. I was feeling good. I had accomplished the shopping I planned, and I'd had a pleasant day away from the tensions of Wisteria. I got out. "Well, here I am," I said, taking his arm. "Back safely without even even a dent in your fender."

He didn't smile. "I wasn't worried about the car," he said. "As for being back safely—I'm not so sure about that."

"What do you mean?"

"Myra had a telephone call from a friend of hers, Amelia St. John. She said she saw you and Jim having lunch together."

We were still standing by the car, and I leaned against it, feeling suddenly weak. "It was my idea," I said quickly. "I ran into him just at lunch time, and it seemed a natural thing to do."

"Natural? My God, what could you be thinking of?"

I looked toward the house, anything to get away from the accusing look in Alex's eyes. I was surprised to see a movement at the window in Alex's office. Someone was watching us. Perhaps listening too? I spoke in a lower tone. "I guess I was thinking that Jim was my friend. And yours. Surely you can't think there was anything wrong."

"Wrong? Oh, I see. No, not that way. But you're white, and he's black. Didn't you think about that?"

"No, but Jim did. He told me people in Abbeville wouldn't approve." But I had thought it wouldn't matter because no one would see us. Suddenly my fine gesture seemed not quite so brave.

"Tracy, you don't understand how things are down here. We have certain customs we've lived with for hundreds of years. You can't come here and change them overnight."

"I wasn't trying to force my ways on anyone else," I said slowly, "but I have to be honest about what I believe. Don't you see, Alex? If I hadn't gone to lunch with Jim just because Abbeville doesn't approve, I would have denied my own principles."

"What about Jim?" he said. "Didn't it occur to you that you might be embarrassing him? That maybe you talked him into it against his will, that he didn't feel free to turn your invitation down? I've known Jim all my life, and we understand each other. He believes in our customs the same as I do. He would never have invited you to lunch, and when you invited him, he probably didn't know how to deal with the situation. You weren't fair to him, Tracy."

"I don't think he accepted out of social awkwardness," I said, rejecting Alex's reasoning. "Jim seems perfectly capable of managing any situation. No, he wanted to come. He likes me, and he knows I like him. He thought, as I did, that there was nothing wrong with friends having lunch together, even if one was black and the other white."

"I doubt if you understand Jim as well as you think you do."

"And I doubt if *you* understand him as well as you think you do."

He stared at me, and I stared back. it seemed to me that I had been apologizing for something ever since I came here. This was one thing I wouldn't apologize for. Perhaps I wasn't as brave as I thought, lunching with Jim. I hadn't expected to be seen. But now that I had been, I wouldn't make excuses.

"Amelia St. John will tell this all over town," Alex said. "But fortunately, everybody knows her reputation for gossip, so a lot of what she says will be discounted."

"That's a cowardly way out, Alex. I *did* lunch with Jim."

He kept looking at me. Finally he said, "If you're going to defy the whole town, you'll have to count me out. I don't care to get involved in battles that seem unnecessary."

Suddenly I felt young and uncertain. "Jim said something like that, too. But I still don't see—"

He sighed. "Maybe I'm wrong, Tracy. You and I belong to different generations."

I took his arm. The argument seemed unimportant compared to the distance Alex was putting between us. "No, don't say that. I don't want you to think of the years between us. I'm as old as you are in every way that counts. I can't feel as you do about this, but that doesn't mean we can't work it out. Jim said sometimes it is necessary to compromise—"

Alex said in a slow, thoughtful way, "I don't want you to change, Tracy. I fell in love with you the way you are. Maybe your relationship with Jim won't be what I expected, but I'll leave that up to you. I should have thought this through before I talked to you, but Myra was so upset—"

Myra again. I looked back toward the windows of Alex's office, but they were blank; nothing moved behind them. I thought it quite likely that it had been Myra standing there. She had laid the fuse to dynamite; she would have wanted to hear the explosion.

But when we went in, Myra was nowhere to be seen. Britt was coming down the stairs dressed in his riding clothes. Answering my question, he said, "Myra? She's at a Red Cross meeting. . . . I thought I'd ride, Alex, if you aren't going to use Toffy."

I looked after him thoughtfully. I couldn't think of any reason Britt would have for eaves-dropping on us.

Chapter 10

One of Pam's friends was giving a party for Alex and me, a barbecue on the patio. There must have been fifty people present. Most of them I had met before, and by slow degrees I was beginning to know them by name.

Alex and I moved around, chatting with people. Alex did most of the talking, while I concentrated on remembering names and trying to file away in my mind details about them. I thought it was strange how our roles had changed. I was naturally more talkative than Alex; I found it quite easy to carry on long conversations on almost any subject. But when it came to making small talk, I was struck dumb. I didn't know any of the details of these people's lives, and once the weather was disposed of, I couldn't think of anything to say. I smiled pleasantly and called those I could remember by name and hoped Alex wouldn't find me stupid and dull. He chatted easily with everyone and seemed to remember everything about them, the names of their children, the kinds of work they did, the makes of their cars, where they had gone on vacation. Yet, as I knew, Alex wasn't very good at talking about the things that really mattered in his own life.

I was talking with the hostess, June Redfern. With the serving finished and all her guests taken care of, she had come over and sat down at the table with Alex and me.

June and I talked on. Alex didn't come back. I didn't see him on the patio, and I wondered where he was. After a while, June said, "They've been playing that record for the past thirty minutes. I'll see if it's the only one they can find."

She left. No one else was close by, and I thought that soon I would have to move and begin talking to someone else. But for the moment it was a relief to be alone, not to have to smile and try to think of something to say. While I was still sitting there, Myra came up and said, "Tracy, I'm not feeling well, but I don't want June to know, or she'll think it was the food. Would you bring my purse out of the den? I have some tablets to settle my stomach."

"Of course. You sit right here, and I'll be back in a jiffy. Oh—where is the den?"

"Just go through that door at the end of the

patio, and you'll be in it. My purse is on the chair by the door."

I opened the door, stepped inside—and stopped still. Straight ahead of me on the other side of the room a man and woman were in odd embrace. Evidently he had walked up behind her and put his arms around her. Their backs were to me, and I could see nothing of the woman but the top of her head. She had brown hair. I had no idea who she was. But I knew the man. It was Alex.

I turned quickly and stepped back outside the door. Crossing the terrace I held myself back from a run. But even so, my feet hurried, clicking across the pavement. I passed by Myra, and she said, "Tracy?" But I did not stop. I couldn't let her see how upset I was, face her questions, tell her what I had seen.

I got to Alex's car. Fortunately, he had parked on the street, so it was not blocked in. But I had no key. Then I thought of the extra key in the magnetized metal box under the hood. In another minute I was away from the curb and headed down the street. I was going to cry. My throat ached. But no tears came into my burning eyes.

I didn't know where I was going. My only thought was to get away from the hateful sight of Alex holding another woman in his arms. Away from that dreadful farce that pretended to be a party in my honor. With their intimate knowledge of each other's lives, everyone in town must know that Alex was in love with someone else. They had been watching me, wondering when I would find out, how I would take it. He could have told her that he did not love me, that he was marrying me for my money. I was a fool to think he hadn't known about it. She might have agreed to Alex's marrying me. Maybe he did not mean to break off with her at all; he would be married to me, but he would love her.

Or perhaps he did not love her either. My heart chilled. Could he be playing with her, too? Was Alex that sort of man, a philanderer? An old-fashioned word, that. An old-fashioned word for an old sin.

I was trembling; my teeth were clicking together, and I could hardly keep my hands on the wheel. It was dangerous to drive in such a state. I would have to stop until I got hold of myself. I turned into the first driveway I saw and stopped the car. Only then did I realize I was in front of Jim's house. Apparently, I had unconsciously taken the road to Wisteria, since it was the only one I knew.

After a minute Jim came out of the house and walked to the car. "Oh, it's you, Tracy. I recognized Alex's car."

I didn't say anything. He leaned forward to look at me and said, "What's wrong?"

I couldn't tell him. My teeth chattered, and my shoulders shook, and not a word would come. He opened the door and got me up the walk. Inside he said crisply, "Sit there." I sat down in the big soft chair and shook and shook. Jim left the room and came back with a steaming mug. "Drink this," he said.

It was coffee, black and hot and bitter. My chattering teeth clicked against the rim of the cup, and it shook in my hands. Jim took it from me and held it to my mouth as one holds a cup for a child. "Now tell me about it," he said.

I found that my trembling had almost stopped, and I could talk again. By degrees I told him what had happened.

He said slowly, "Mrs. Farrington sent you into the den?"

For a minute I was blank. "Mrs. Farrington? Oh. Yes, it was Myra. You think she meant for me to see Alex and the woman?"

I stared at the empty cup on the coffee table as if it were a crystal ball in which I could see the entire scene. Perhaps Myra had seen it first. She could have known what I would see in the den. "I don't understand Myra," I said, "She's very cordial on the surface, but underneath she resents me. I don't know why, unless she wants to keep everything as it is."

"I hardly think that," he said in a dry voice.

"What else could it be?"

"Mrs. Farrington is a pretty woman," he said obliquely. "And still young—she and Alex are about the same age. They share the same concerns —the house, the children, the affairs of the town."

"What are you getting at?"

For a moment he didn't answer. His dark eyes shifted, going around the room and finally resting on my face again. He seemed unwilling to speak. Finally he said, "After Roy died, I wondered if they would marry."

I was silent. Strange, that hadn't occurred to me before. I had thought Myra was fearful that I would supplant her as mistress of Wisteria, but I had not dreamed she wanted to marry Alex herself. I thought back, considering what I had seen of their relationship in the light of what Jim was suggesting. There had been nothing between them. Nothing. Except that one glance I had seen Alex give her when I said perhaps someone was trying to keep me from marrying him.

"Did you have any reason for thinking they might marry?" I asked slowly. "I see that it would have been convenient. But they may not have considered it."

He still seemed embarrassed. He doesn't like talking about Alex like this, I thought. Perhaps he feels disloyal. He said in a rush of words, as if in a hurry to get this over, "I don't know how Alex felt about Mrs. Farrington. I thought maybe he was only trying to help her through a lonely time after his brother died. But I saw enough to know she was after him."

I said in a dull voice, "It doesn't matter. Even if Myra did send me to the den knowing what I would see, there's still the fact that Alex was there with another woman. That was Alex's action, not Myra's."

Jim's eyes behind their glasses were unhappy. After a moment he said, "It may be a good thing you saw it if it sends you away from Wisteria. There's danger for you there, Tracy, real danger. And not from Mrs. Farrington."

"Who then?"

He shook his head. "I wish I knew. But I'm sure

it wasn't Mrs. Farrington who tried to drown you. She is too devious for that."

"Devious, yes, that describes Myra."

"Trying to drown you was a bold action. It took someone with a strong nerve and a lot of daring."

"But there has to be a reason. Why would anyone—except possibly Myra—want to kill me?"

"How can you tell what seems a good reason to a murderer? I'm relieved to know you're leaving. You and Alex can work out the—the misunderstanding, I'm sure, and maybe by then things will have changed at Wisteria. Nothing ever stays the same, Tracy. That's one thing you can depend on."

"I must go," I said. "Thanks for letting me talk. I was in quite a state when I stopped here, but I feel better now."

"I'm glad I could help. Will you be all right? Would you like me to drive you?"

"No, I'm fine. Thanks again."

I was surprised to see that Myra's car was not in the driveway. I had thought they would be home. But when I got to the light on the front porch, I looked at my watch and saw that it was only eleven. It seemed longer since I had left the party. Evidently my leaving hadn't broken it up. Probably no one had noticed I was gone.

I hesitated, not wanting to enter the house alone. While I stood there, Chris came to the door. In his hand he held a glass half full of a brownish liquid, whiskey from the meal. He looked at me in surprise. "I heard the car. Where are the others?"

"The party isn't over," I answered. "I left early."

He was walking down the hall in front of me. His head jerked around. "What happened? Was it Myra? Oh, don't look so surprised. I can see what's going on. Myra means to keep Alex from marrying you. The same way she tried to keep Pam from marrying me. Myra wants to own people."

He walked into the living room while he was talking, and I followed him. "Pam *did* marry you," I pointed out.

He sighed and looked at the glass he was holding. His square, stocky figure looked curiously small. I hadn't realized before that he was no taller than I. "She married me," he said, "but you notice she hasn't got away from Myra. Would you like a drink?"

I shook my head. He emptied his and poured another from the tray on a nearby table. He sat down, slumped against the cushions. "Don't worry," he said. "I'm not drunk. I've been home only a half hour. I started to come to the party, but I was so tired I decided to rebel for once."

"Rebel?"

"Against the life Myra plans for us. I usually do what she wants, but I don't know how much longer I can take it. I work hard, and I would like to rest, get some exercise, and catch up on the medical journals when I'm home. Myra doesn't give me much chance. There's always a party or a committee meeting or something. Tonight I didn't feel like facing it."

"But surely if you told Pam how you feel—"

He smiled cynically. "You think I haven't? She makes an effort—for a day or two. Then Myra has something else for us to do, and Myra is always right, in Pam's sight."

"You'll be —in your own home soon."

"I don't know. She can't make a decision without consulting Myra, and Myra has already started pointing out the defects. It's happening again just as it has before."

"But Pam was so crazy about the Evans place. I can't believe she'll change her mind that easily."

"Then you don't know her. The slightest hint from Myra is Pam's command. She worships Myra. Why do you think I'm practicing in Abbeville?"

"I knew you came here because it's Pam's home, but I thought you liked it, too."

He shrugged. "I planned to practice in Atlanta, but Pam was miserable there. She visited here so often I finally decided if I wanted to see anything of her, we'd have to move."

"In time, she would have grown away from home, surely. After all, she married you."

"Because she thought she had to." He laughed harshly. "Don't look so shocked. I knew she loved me, but she shied away from marriage, kept refusing to set a date. So finally I persuaded her to spend a weekend with me. Afterward, I convinced her she was pregnant. It was the only way I could get her." He paused and then said simply, "I had to have her."

He finished his drink and set the glass down. "Maybe I am a little drunk. But I wanted you to know what you're up against. The best thing you could do is get married right away, because the longer you wait, the more schemes she'll think up to keep you apart . . . Is that a car I hear?"

"I don't hear it . . . Yes, I do."

As the sound got nearer, Chris got up. "I'm tired, Tracy, and angry, too. If I stay, I may say something I'll be sorry for. Will you tell them I've gone to bed?"

I nodded, and he went down the hall toward the stairs. His footsteps sounded slow and heavy, like an old man's.

I was in the hall when they came in. I spoke before anyone had time to say anything. "Pam, Chris was tired and went to bed. Alex, I want to talk to you. Where shall we go?"

"To my office?"

I walked ahead of him, leaving Myra standing in the hall looking after us. Alex shut the door, and I said immediately, "I'm leaving here tonight. I suppose there is a hotel I can go to?"

"I'll be glad to take you there," he said in a tight voice. "But before you go, would you mind telling me what this is about? June knocked herself out to give a party for you, and then you left right in the middle of it. To go to see Jim, of all things."

"How did you know that?"

"You should know by now that nothing is a secret here. You were seen." I saw that he was furious, trying to hold himself in. He, furious with me.

I flashed angrily, "What if I did go to Jim's? You said our relationship was our own business. And I needed to see him."

"Needed to see him? *Needed* to see him? Just what is your relationship?"

Cold fury engulfed me at what I thought he was implying. "He's my friend," I cried. "The only friend I have here."

"If he is, it's your own fault. Everyone has tried to be friendly with you."

"I've been insulted in a hundred subtle ways and frightened out of my wits by a ghost. You and Myra arranged my wedding without considering what I wanted. One of my most valued possessions has been stolen. And someone tried to kill me. If you call that friendly, then I guess your standards are different from mine."

His face looked shocked. "But, good Lord, you make it sound so malevolent. I know a lot of things have happened, but—"

"Too many, Alex. They couldn't all be accidents. There is something evil here. But that wouldn't have made me leave. I would have stayed and tried to find out what the evil was. I would have tried to fight it. But when I found you didn't love me—I can't fight that."

"You found I didn't love you? What are you talking about?"

"The woman you were with in the den at June's."

"Why, I wasn't—"

"Please don't lie to me, Alex. I saw you. When I went to get Myra's purse, you were standing behind her with your arms around her."

A light of understanding broke over his face, and he laughed. "Oh, that. That was Althea Jones. She had been grading papers all afternoon and had a crick in her neck and shoulders. Myra called me in and asked if I would do what she calls my magic. You must have walked in while I was trying to get the crick out."

"I don't understand."

"Here, I'll show you. Stand in front of me, cross your arms over your chest, and put your fingertips on your shoulders."

I did as he said, and he wrapped his arms around me, holding my left elbow with his right hand and my right elbow with his left. He said, "Then I sort of jounce you, and if the pain is in your shoulders and middle back, it usually relieves it. There's another maneuver for pain in the neck and upper shoulders. I tried both of them on Althea, but you must have seen the one I showed you."

I knew he was right. The position he showed me was exactly the same I had seen him in earlier. I said humbly, "I'm sorry, Alex. But I was so sure—it looked like a particularly tender embrace, the sort of thing a husband or lover would do. I couldn't face anyone right then. I left in your car and started shaking and stopped at Jim's. He took me inside and gave me some hot coffee. I must have been there about an hour."

"Our quarrel over Jim must have left me more on edge than I realized. When Myra told me you had left the party and gone to his house—"

"Myra! She must have followed me!"

"It was natural, wasn't it, to be concerned when she saw you run away?"

I doubted if concern for me was Myra's motive,

but I didn't say anything. He had his arms around me, and I was so glad to have him back again that I could even forget Myra's malicious interference.

After a while Alex said, "What did you mean when you said Myra and I arranged your wedding?"

"When she enlarged the plans and put off the date, you agreed with her. Without even giving me a chance to talk to you."

"I thought it was what you wanted. I didn't want to rush you."

"Alex, why don't we get married this weekend, as we planned? We could have the wedding Sunday afternoon here at Wisteria with Pam and Sandra for bridesmaids. I've already bought their dresses, and mine will be ready Friday. That's the day Grandfather is coming. I never did write him about the change. Oh, I know we could do it, Alex, if you're willing."

The way he kissed me left no doubt of how he felt.

Chapter 11

Breakfast was scorched bacon, overcooked eggs, and soggy toast. Nobody ate much. Myra sighed and said, "I don't know what to do about Mrs. Gilbert. She says if we don't find the cameo, she'll have to leave at the end of the week."

"I don't see that her leaving will solve anything," Alex said.

"She says she can't work here, knowing we suspect her. I wish we hadn't made such a fuss about it." Her eyes flicked over me. It was plain that she was blaming me for the domestic crisis.

Alex sighed. "Do you want me to talk to her again?"

"No, I'll try to soothe her."

He left, and she turned to me. "Tracy, we simply

must make the wedding arrangements today. The way you've been putting it off anyone would think you didn't want to get married."

She stopped, expectantly. I thought, she is waiting for me to tell her we've called off the wedding and I'm leaving. Naturally she would think that after the little scene she had arranged for my benefit last night. Yet in the back of my mind was still a tiny doubt about Myra. She resented me, I knew. But I wasn't sure her resentment was the only reason she was trying to prevent my marriage. The horrible legends she told were true; Alex admitted that, and so did Jim. And the ghost was real. I had seen it.

I trusted Alex. I wouldn't let myself think of those other things. I said, "Yes, we must make the arrangements this morning. Alex and I have decided to be married Sunday afternoon."

She looked nonplussed. After a moment she said in a weak voice, "But that's only three days away. You can't possibly get everything done by then."

"Oh, I think we can. I brought Pam and Sandra's dresses home Tuesday, and mine will be ready Friday. If you still want a reception, I'll have a caterer from the city."

She seemed momentarily at a loss for words. Then she said, "That will be terribly expensive."

Britt was watching our faces. I wondered where his sympathies lay, or if he had any.

"Don't worry about my expense, Myra," I said, "After all, I'll get married only once."

Pam didn't seem to be listening to us but sat silently with her eyes on her plate. Chris said, "Time for me to go," and for a moment his eyes rested on Pam with a bleak look. She didn't raise her eyes, but after he went out, she suddenly got up and followed him. I wondered if they were quarreling about the house.

Britt left shortly afterward, but Myra and I sat on at the table. I was telling her about the plans for the wedding.

"Yes, it sounds fine," she said, "I'm sure everything will work out. Are you going on a wedding trip?"

"No, Alex doesn't feel he can get away now. He said we would take a long trip later, perhaps in the fall."

"I think you should persuade him to go away now, if only for a day or two. You see, he and Elizabeth didn't."

"And you think he'll be thinking of her?"

"It would be natural. But no, I wasn't thinking of that. I was thinking that away from here Alex might not be so obsessed with tradition."

I said, proud that my voice sounded so calm, "The mark of the Farringtons again? Don't be ridiculous, Myra."

"No woman knows a man until after she marries him," she said darkly.

"Perhaps not, but at least I know Alex better than that."

She sighed. "Ah, the romantic dreams of youth. I wonder if you know how young you seem to me. But then, Alex likes his women young. Did you know Elizabeth wasn't even as old as you are?

Nineteen when they married, twenty when she died."

I refused to let her get me upset. I might be young, but I could be mature beyond my years. I would be calm and unemotional, show Myra nothing was to be gained by throwing Alex's first marriage in my face. I said, "Yes, I knew she lived only a year. I don't think anyone said what she died of though."

"I'm not quite sure," Myra said slowly. "I don't believe the doctor was either, although he must have put something natural and unsuspicious on the death certificate."

My calm was swept away. I swallowed. "Are you saying her death wasn't natural?"

Myra's eyes shifted. "It isn't natural for a twenty-year-old girl to die, is it?"

"But she was sick. Jim said so. He said she was in and out of the hospital. She must have had some disease, and it seems you would know what it was, living here in the same house."

"I'm sorry, but I don't. I wondered, of course, but Alex never told me. The police never questioned anybody, and they would have if the doctor had reported anything odd . . ." Her voice trailed off. She seemed to be thinking back to the past, questioning. Then she got up and said briskly, "Well, I can't sit here all morning. I must see if I can smooth Mrs. Gilbert's ruffled feathers."

I was puzzled by Myra's revelations. It seemed very odd that she did not know the cause of Elizabeth's death. But as she said, sometimes people were reticent about illness especially if it was

Of All Brands Sold: Lowest tar: 2 mg. "tar," 0.2 mg. nicotine av. per cigarette, FTC Report Apr. 1976.
Kent Golden Lights: 8 mg. "tar," 0.7 mg. nicotine av. per cigarette by FTC Method.

NEW!
KENT GOLDEN LIGHTS LOWER IN TAR THAN ALL THESE BRANDS.

Non-menthol Filter Brands	Tar	Nicotine	Non-menthol Filter Brands	Tar	Nicotine
KENT GOLDEN LIGHTS	**8 mg.**	**0.7 mg.***	RALEIGH 100's	17 mg.	1.2 mg.
MERIT	9 mg.	0.7 mg.*	MARLBORO 100's	17 mg.	1.1 mg.
VANTAGE	11 mg.	0.7 mg.	BENSON & HEDGES 100's	18 mg.	1.1 mg.
MULTIFILTER	13 mg.	0.8 mg.	VICEROY 100's	18 mg.	1.2 mg.
WINSTON LIGHTS	13 mg.	0.9 mg.	MARLBORO KING SIZE	18 mg.	1.1 mg.
MARLBORO LIGHTS	13 mg.	0.8 mg.	LARK	18 mg.	1.2 mg.
RALEIGH EXTRA MILD	14 mg.	0.9 mg.	CAMEL FILTERS	18 mg.	1.2 mg.
VICEROY EXTRA MILD	14 mg.	0.9 mg.	EVE	18 mg.	1.2 mg.
PARLIAMENT BOX	14 mg.	0.8 mg.	WINSTON 100's	18 mg.	1.2 mg.
DORAL	15 mg.	1.0 mg.	WINSTON BOX	18 mg.	1.2 mg.
PARLIAMENT KING SIZE	16 mg.	0.9 mg.	CHESTERFIELD	19 mg.	1.2 mg.
VICEROY	16 mg.	1.1 mg.	LARK 100's	19 mg.	1.2 mg.
RALEIGH	16 mg.	1.1 mg.	L&M KING SIZE	19 mg.	1.2 mg.
VIRGINIA SLIMS	16 mg.	1.0 mg.	TAREYTON 100's	19 mg.	1.4 mg.
PARLIAMENT 100's	17 mg.	1.0 mg.	WINSTON KING SIZE	19 mg.	1.3 mg.
L&M BOX	17 mg.	1.1 mg.	L&M 100's	19 mg.	1.3 mg.
SILVA THINS	17 mg.	1.3 mg.	PALL MALL 100's	19 mg.	1.4 mg.
MARLBORO BOX	17 mg.	1.0 mg.	TAREYTON	21 mg.	1.4 mg.

Source: FTC Report Apr. 1976
*By FTC Method

> Warning: The Surgeon General Has Determined That Cigarette Smoking Is Dangerous to Your Health.

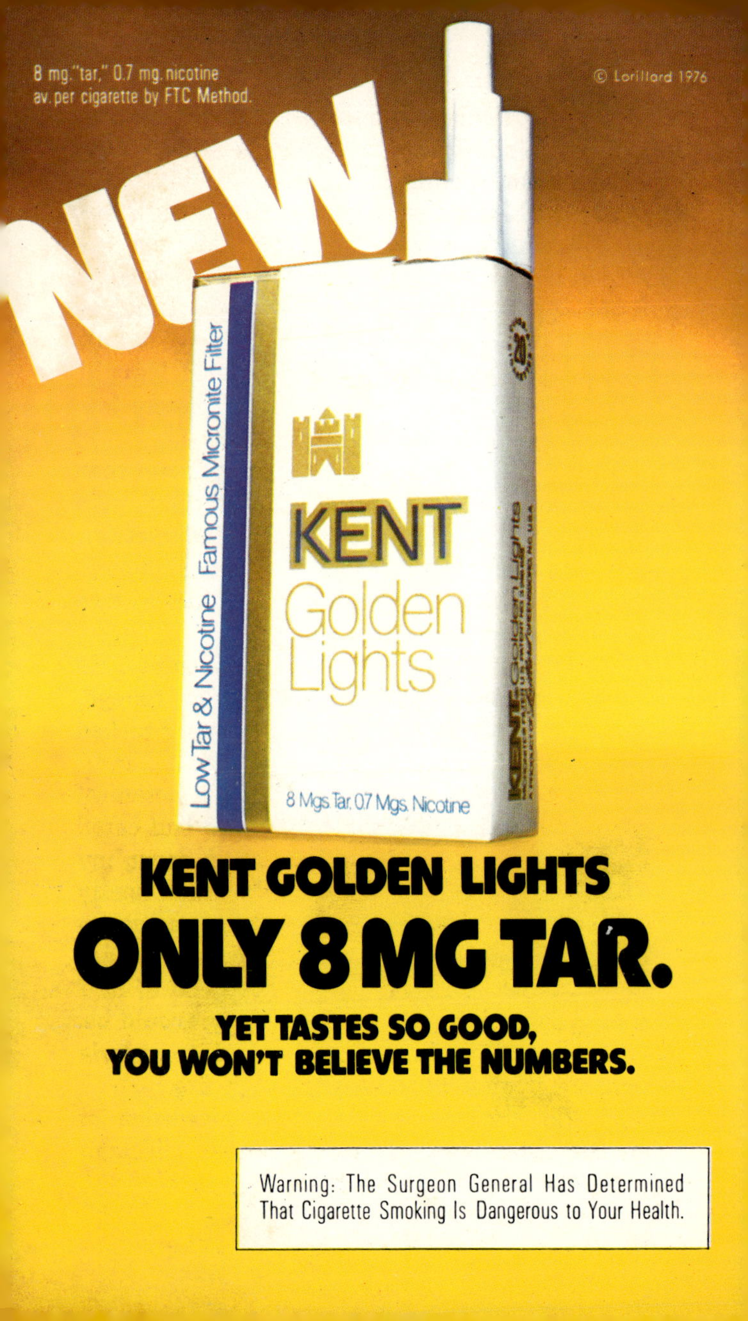
8 mg."tar," 0.7 mg. nicotine
av. per cigarette by FTC Method.
© Lorillard 1976
NEW
Low Tar & Nicotine Famous Micronite Filter
KENT
Golden
Lights
8 Mgs. Tar. 0.7 Mgs. Nicotine
KENT GOLDEN LIGHTS
ONLY 8 MG TAR.
YET TASTES SO GOOD,
YOU WON'T BELIEVE THE NUMBERS.
Warning: The Surgeon General Has Determined
That Cigarette Smoking Is Dangerous to Your Health.

something particularly painful or horrible. I put it out of my mind. The past was gone. I must help Alex forget those painful memories.

I borrowed Alex's car and went to town. I regretted having sold mine, although Alex had encouraged me to, saying that his would always be available to me. Besides, he said, there were already too many cars at Wisteria; the garage wasn't big enough for all of them. But I decided I would buy one later anyway. I didn't feel completely free to borrow Alex's so often.

In spite of Myra's dire predictions, I found that Mrs. Johnson, the florist, was free to do the flowers for the wedding. I also went by to see the minister, called a caterer, and then did a little shopping. When I got back to Wisteria I went to Alex's office to tell him everything was all set.

The door was open, but the office was empty. He must have stepped out for only a minute though, because the desk was covered with papers. I picked up a framed picture and saw that it was a blown-up snapshot of me, taken one day in the botanical garden at school. I was pleased that he had cared enough to frame it. As I set the picture down, my hand brushed against a container in which neatly sharpened pencils stood upright. There was something else in the container, a steel rod about a foot long with a flat piece of metal on the end of it. I picked it up curiously, wondering what it could be. There was a raised design on the end, a wisteria bloom, not shiny but blackened, as if by fire.

My skin prickled with sudden knowledge of what the object was. My hands turned cold, and

129

my forehead was hot. Saliva ran too freely in my mouth, and I kept swallowing, hoping my heaving stomach would stop. I ran for the bathroom down the hall and splashed cold water on my face and held a wet towel against my throat. At last my stomach quieted, but I felt weak and shaken. After a moment I went toward the stairs. I thought I heard the door to the office close, but I didn't look around. I didn't want to see Alex now.

Somehow I got through the rest of the afternoon. I was even glad to learn there was another party in my honor, although I cared little about parties, especially in a town where everyone knew each other and I knew nobody. But this one would put off my having to face Alex with what I had seen this afternoon, and for that I was grateful.

After the party, Britt went off to meet Sandra's plane; they would be late getting to Abbeville. The rest of us went home and to our rooms. Alex would have detained me, I think, but I told him I was tired. It was only partly true. I still wasn't ready to face him. I couldn't believe what I was thinking, and yet I had seen the object with my own eyes, even held it in my hand.

I woke with the familiar prickling at the base of my scalp and saw the ghost. It was darker in the room than it had been the other times. I could see only a vague blur of white. A moving blur. The ghost was coming toward me. I screamed then and screamed and screamed.

The light went on. The room was empty except for Alex in his pajamas looking at me with frightened eyes.

"The ghost," I cried. "It was here again."

He put his arms around me. "You're all right. Tracy, you're all *right*. Whatever it was is gone."

"Did you see it? Was it still here when you came?"

He shook his head.

Pam and Chris appeared in the doorway. "What's wrong?" Chris asked.

Alex hesitated. I said, "I saw a ghost."

"Saw a *what?*" Pam asked.

"A ghost. In my room."

"You must have been dreaming," Chris said. He shrugged. "A ghost is out of my line, and I was up at five this morning. I'm going back to bed."

He left, but Pam came in the room. Myra followed her, a bit out of breath but her usual well-groomed self in a long black velvet robe. Britt came in, too. Excitedly they shot questions at me.

Alex said, "Can't you see she's too frightened to talk now? Here, Tracy, put this on. All of you get dressed, and we'll go downstairs. This isn't the first time someone has been in Tracy's room, and I want to get to the bottom of it."

"Now, Tracy," Alex said when we were all seated, "tell us what you saw tonight."

I described the ghost as best I could. Alex's face was grim and angry; Pam and Myra were horrified. Britt looked as if something puzzling had suddenly been explained. He said, "So that's what—"

He broke off. Alex said, "What were you going to say, Britt?"

"That's what has been bothering Tracy. I knew

there was something. No wonder she had shadows under her eyes."

I don't think that was what he had started to say. I wondered if he knew something about the ghost, or if he had seen it himself. But he said no more.

"The way you describe what you saw, it sounds like Elizabeth, Alex's first wife," Myra said. She shivered. "Do you suppose her spirit is upset because Alex is marrying again?"

"That's nonsense," Pam cried. She looked around the circle of faces. "Isn't it?" she asked in an uncertain voice.

Pam frowned. "Can a ghost actually do anything? I mean, they don't have real bodies, do they? They're just visions, sort of."

"Exactly," Alex said grimly. "So if a ghost isn't trying to harm Tracy, who is? Don't forget she almost drowned."

They all looked at me. "Wait a minute, Alex," Britt said. "Are you accusing one of us of trying to kill Tracy? That's too ridiculous to talk about."

"Then how can you explain all that has happened?" Alex asked.

Britt looked thoughtful. I saw a new expression come into his face, a shrewd, cunning look. However, it disappeared quickly, and he was himself again. "Maybe it is a ghost," he said. "I've never thought much about such things, but in one of my psychology courses in college we talked about psychic phenomena. The professor said that so far no one has proved there aren't any ghosts. Could it be Elizabeth, as Myra said?"

"What are we going to do?" Pam asked.

Britt shrugged. "What can we do? There's no protection against a ghost. Except to give it what it wants."

Pam stared at him in shocked dismay. "But it wants Tracy!"

"No, apparently it wants Tracy not to marry Alex. After all, she wasn't bothered by a ghost before she came here. Were you, Tracy?"

Alex looked suddenly tired; the lines in his face all pulled downward and his eyes were bleak and old. "I think you're right, Britt," he said. "We'll have to call off the wedding plans. For the present, at least."

"But, Alex—" I wanted to tell him this wasn't the right thing to do. If we gave in to whatever force was opposing us, we would never be able to marry and live peacefully. We should find out what this was and overcome it.

Alex said in a final voice, "The wedding is off for now. I can't have your life endangered. We'll talk about it tomorrow and make whatever arrangements are necessary. It's late. We should get back to bed. . . . Can you shoot, Tracy?"

"Yes. Grandfather taught me one vacation."

"I'm going to give you a pistol. If anything comes into your room again, I want you to blast away at it."

My thoughts were a turmoil as I went to bed the second time that night. Alex had called off our wedding—for the present, he said. I was beginning to think he didn't *want* to marry me. If he didn't believe in ghosts, why did he allow one to rule our lives? Could it be that he did believe? Did he have some reason to believe?

What kind of man had I promised to marry?

At any rate, if the ghost came back, I had a gun. It was odd how much safer that made me feel. Because after all a gun is no protection against a ghost.

Chapter 12

Alex had already finished breakfast when I got down. Chris and Britt were gone, too, but Pam and Myra were still at the table.

"How do you feel this morning?" Pam asked.

"Fine. I wasn't sure I would be able to sleep, but I did. Like a log."

"I didn't," Myra said. "I was nervous all night. I kept waking up expecting to see a ghost in my room. Now that I know about it, I think I'll jump at every noise for a month. But it was best to tell us. You can't face a horror like that alone. I must admit I was surprised at Alex's calling off the wedding so readily. It almost seems as if—but that's ridiculous. The ghost couldn't be his fault. I mean, even if it is Elizabeth, Alex has nothing to do with her coming back." She paused.

My mind flew to the object I had seen yesterday. But I turned my thoughts. I would not think of that horrible story any more. What I saw was a—a letter sealer. Something to make an impression in sealing wax. It had nothing to do with the mark of the Farringtons.

"I think Alex is right to call off the wedding," Pam said. "It isn't for always, only until we know more about whatever is going on."

"What will you do now?" Myra asked me. "You're welcome to stay here as long as you like."

"I don't know until I talk to Alex," I said. "I'll see him now."

He looked up from the papers on his desk. "Do you mind waiting a moment? I need to answer this right away."

I sat on the sofa and waited while he made a telephone call. My eyes were irresistibly drawn to the pencil holder on the desk. I wanted to ask him about it before I left. I wanted to hear him say the object was a letter sealer.

But today it was gone; the container held nothing but pencils.

Alex hung up the phone and came to sit on the sofa beside me. He took my hands. "You understand why we have to delay our wedding, don't you? I don't want to, but I'm afraid of what may happen if we don't. I can't gamble with your safety."

"Yes, I understand that. But what do we do now?"

"Your grandfather is coming tonight, isn't he?"

"Yes, but he hasn't left yet. I can call him and tell him not to come."

"There's no use getting him upset. Let him come, and when he gets here, we'll tell him we've decided to put the ceremony off till next week."

"Perhaps you should tell the family not to mention the ghost. I'm not anxious to tell Grandfather about that. You'll know why when you meet him."

"Then it's all settled."

I didn't say anything, but I couldn't see that. Nothing was solved by equivocation.

"What are you staring at?" Alex asked.

"Your pencil holder. Yesterday when I was in here there was a letter sealer in it."

"A letter sealer?"

"A device for making an impression on sealing wax. It had a wisteria bloom on it."

"Oh, yes, Myra gave me one at Christmas one year. I don't think I ever used it, and I had no idea it was still around."

"Yesterday it was in the pencil holder."

"No, it wouldn't be there. It's too small to stand up in the holder."

"Too small? It was taller than the pencils."

"If it was, it wasn't mine."

"Whose then?"

He frowned. "I don't know. No one else uses this office. Why are you so concerned about a letter sealer?"

I couldn't say, Because it looked like a branding iron. I didn't want to see Alex's face turn dark; I didn't want him to turn his fierce anger on me.

137

But all the same I did say it. Because I wanted even less to have these nauseating suspicions of Alex. Every time I convinced myself they weren't true, some new piece of evidence turned up to refute my conviction. If there was nothing sinister about the letter sealer, why had Alex removed it from the pencil holder?

He didn't say anything at first. He stood looking at me, his body stiff and a black frown on his face. I braced myself for an explosion. But it didn't come. Instead he asked in a soft, dangerous voice, "Do you believe that, Tracy?"

"No." Then I said in a voice thick with misery. "I don't believe it. I can't. And yet—it was on your desk yesterday, and now it's gone. And I do have the feeling that you're still bound to Elizabeth. You can't talk about her; even the mention of her name ties you in knots. I can't help wondering if there is something"—I paused and then my words came in a rush—"some promise perhaps that you feel guilty about breaking. Some promise Elizabeth won't let you break."

He turned his back on me. My shoulders slumped. The room seemed darker, as if the sun had gone behind a cloud.

I straightened my shoulders. "Alex," I said urgently. "I love you. Even if you did—something horrible fifteen years ago, I love you. Everybody makes mistakes. All I need is to hear you say it *was* a mistake."

He turned and looked straight at me. "You'll never hear me say that," he said harshly, "because I've never had any part in such perverted nonsense. But you are right about one thing. I do feel guilty about Elizabeth."

My breath was cut off. He was staring at me and yet beyond me into some realm where I could not follow. I thought soon he would begin talking again and take me into his troubled past.

Instead his eyes suddenly focused on my face, and he said, "Myra tells me she is having another swimming party this afternoon. Tracy, if you go in, I want to be right beside you. Let's not take any chances."

"All right, Alex."

A plan which had been developing in my mind a long time suddenly unfolded. I couldn't help feeling it was disloyal to Alex, but I told myself resentfully that it was his own fault. He had been far from frank with me. "Is it all right if I use your car?" I asked. "I'll buy one when I get to town and have them bring yours back."

If I was going to be disloyal, at least I wouldn't use Alex's car.

"You talk as if you're going to pick up a toothbrush at the drug store. You can't buy a car like that."

"Why not?" I asked, surprised.

He stared at me a moment. Then he shrugged. "No reason, I guess. I keep forgetting you are a rich girl. I have to consider for months before I trade cars."

"But I need one today. I can't consider for months. I've inconvenienced you long enough."

"Well, at least make a show of indecision. Ed

Burney will faint if you go in and say 'I'll take that one.'"

"All right. I'll let him give me a sales talk."

But even so it didn't take long. I tried out a blue Buick and a yellow Chevrolet and bought the Chevrolet because I liked the bright, cheerful color. I left Alex's car with Mr. Burney and drove to Chris's office.

Chris looked different in his white coat. More prepossessing. I shouldn't have come during office hours, I thought nervously. I'm taking his time from truly needy people.

"Hi, Tracy," he said. "My nurse said you wanted to talk to me. There's nothing wrong, I hope?" His gray eyes looked anxious behind their glasses. Suddenly he was Chris again, and I could talk to him. I didn't even have to rush. Today there were no emergencies.

"I wanted to ask you a question," I said. "Perhaps I should have asked Alex, but he doesn't seem to like to talk about his first wife. And no one else seems to know. How did Elizabeth die?"

"I'm afraid I can't tell you. It was long before I came here."

"But you took over the former doctor's practice, didn't you?"

"Yes, Dr. Manning retired. But he was an old-fashioned doctor. He kept all his records in his head. I can't answer your question, I'm afraid. I can find out if you want me to, but it will take a little time."

"This Dr. Manning. You said he retired. Is he still alive then?"

"Yes, he's in a rest home in the city. Clayton Convalescent Home on the highway."

"Do they have visiting hours every day? Do you think I could see him?"

"Yes, but is it that important? Surely Myra could tell you if you don't want to ask Alex."

"I have to go to town anyway; they promised to have my wedding dress ready today. I can stop and talk to Dr. Manning while I'm there."

Chapter 13

My wedding dress was ready. I stood before a mirror while the bridal consultant arranged the gleaming satin folds. "It's a perfect fit," she said. "I was a little afraid something would be wrong, since we had to do it so quickly. But it looks lovely on you."

"Yes," I agreed, turning for a better view. It was beautiful. It made *me* look beautiful. "Such a lovely bride," the women would say. And the men would pound Alex on the back, "Boy, you did all right for yourself."

The vision faded. I wasn't getting married this week. The wedding was indefinitely postponed. I wondered when I would get to wear my beautiful dress, or if I ever would.

I left the store and started toward the convalescent home, feeling dull and depressed. Suddenly I jerked to attention. The car in front was just like Alex's. I peered at it a moment, then relaxed against the car seat, dismissing the thought. There must be thousands of dark blue Buicks here. Alex hadn't mentioned coming to the city today.

But it was Alex in the car ahead; I was sure of it. The back of his dark head, the set of his shoulders—it was Alex. He made a right turn, and I saw the side of his face. There could no longer be any doubt. But where was he going? Perhaps he knew a shortcut to the highway. I turned too and was just about to toot my horn to let him know I was behind when he pulled over to the curb and stopped. I went on by, looking back in the mirror. He got out of the car, looked up and down the street, and went rapidly toward the nearest house, a modest white bungalow on a well-kept lawn.

Who was Alex visiting? He hadn't mentioned having friends or relatives in the city. There was something about the way he searched the street and then hurried into the house, something secret, furtive. I turned at the next corner and parked on the other street. I would see Alex when he went by, and then I could find out where he had been. I waited.

I felt guilty about spying on Alex. I knew there was a perfectly good reason for his visit to the white cottage. I trusted Alex. I would go home now before he came out. But my hands did not reach for the ignition key. I sat there waiting. After a long while, I saw Alex's car go by. My watch told me it had been only forty minutes. After he was out of sight down the street, I drove around the block and stopped in front of the house I had seen him enter.

I hesitated a moment, wondering what I should say to the stranger who would come to the door. Perhaps I could pretend to be selling something. But I was no good at lying. It would be better to tell the truth.

A fat middle-aged woman with black hair and a protuberant stomach came to the door.

"I'm Tracy Meadows, Alex Farrington's fiancée," I said.

Her round face registered surprise. "Glad to meet you," she said. "You just missed Alex; he hasn't been gone five minutes." She looked down the street as if she expected to see his car. Then she looked back at me and said, "Won't you come in?"

The room we stepped into was dominated by a huge television set which showed a colored picture of a doctor and a nurse talking to each other in earnest voices. An elderly woman with short, frizzy gray hair sat on the sofa watching. She was fat and had the same protuberant stomach as the younger woman.

"Mama, is it all right if I turn off the television set?" the younger woman asked.

The other looked up and saw me. "Yes," she said. "There's not much happening today. They're just talking about the operation they are going to do tomorrow."

"Won't you sit down?" the young woman said.

"Mamma, this is Tracy Meadows, Alex's girl friend."

"You just missed Alex," the gray-haired woman said.

I felt confused and wished I hadn't come. I sat on the edge of a big lounge chair and looked about the room. It was furnished with a sofa and chair with plastic end tables and matching lamps. There were thin nylon curtains at the windows, and the floors were bare and highly polished. In the precise center of the small coffee table was a vase of bright pink artificial roses. Everything was scrupulously clean. We sat looking at each other. I said, "It's a hot day, isn't it?"

"Yes, it is hot for this time of year," the younger woman replied. "Dusty, too. You wouldn't believe how often I have to dust in here, even with a paved road outside. I don't know where it comes from."

"It's in the air, I suspect," I said.

We were silent again.

"The roads are awfully dusty around Wisteria," I offered.

"How do you like Wisteria?" the younger woman asked.

"It's a beautiful house," I said.

"Yes, it's pretty, but I'd hate to have the housekeeping. All those rooms—it would take a week to get through them." She looked around with satisfaction on her face.

Seeing her expression, I said, "Everything here looks so clean and polished. It must take a lot of work to keep it this way."

"It's work, but at least I can see what I've done

when I get through. Not like the old place in Abbeville."

"Oh, did you live in Abbeville?"

"A long time ago. We've been here fifteen years. Mama still thinks about the old place, but everything is so much more convenient here. Air conditioning and central heat, even a dishwasher. We're close to a shopping center and a church, too."

"Maybe the old place wasn't so much, but it was home," the old woman said. "And we had neighbors. Here nobody cares whether you live or die."

"Oh, Mamma, you know they've been nice to us. But all the women work; they don't have time to visit."

The old lady turned to me and said in a complaining voice, "I sit here all day, and sometimes I don't see a soul from the time Anna goes to work till she gets home. If it wasn't for the television, I'd go crazy."

"Alex gave her the television last Christmas," the younger woman said. "It's been a big help. It *is* lonesome for her, but what can I do? There's no work to be had in Abbeville."

"What do you do?" I asked.

"Grocery checker at the supermarket. I'll soon be there fifteen years."

"And what has it got you?" the old lady asked. "If it wasn't for what Alex gives us, we couldn't even get by. You'd have done better to get married."

The younger woman flushed and said nothing.

"She could have got married," the old woman said to me. "Anna was pretty as a picture when she

147

was young. Not quite as pretty as Elizabeth but plenty good-looking enough to catch a husband. I dressed them both real well. I used to be a good seamstress before my hands stiffened up."

So this was Elizabeth's mother, this complaining old woman. And the daughter who took care of her was Elizabeth's sister. I looked at her again. Why, she wasn't more than forty, only a little older than Elizabeth would be. If Elizabeth had lived, she might be as fat and ugly as her sister by now. I thought of the lovely girl in the portrait.

"The portrait of Elizabeth at Wisteria is beautiful," I said. "It must have been painted before she got sick."

At last I would find out what Elizabeth had died of. Perhaps I could find out too about the scar. My heart was beating fast as I waited for Mrs. Lavelle's reply.

"That is a pretty picture," she said. "I wanted it, but I wouldn't ask Alex. I knew he wouldn't want to part with it. It was painted soon after she married, almost a year before she passed away. She was already sick, but it didn't show." She paused and then said, "It never did show much. She kept her looks to the last. She never did know what was wrong with her."

"What was her illness?" I asked.

She looked surprised. "Leukemia. Didn't Alex tell you? But then he doesn't talk much about Elizabeth, even to me. He took her death awfully hard."

Leukemia. She must have been sick for years, even before she married.

Mrs. Lavelle said, "The doctor thought we ought

148

to tell her, but I didn't want her to have that hanging over her head to spoil her happiness. They had a month together before she had another flare-up and Alex found out. Then he helped me keep it from her. We gave out all kinds of excuses for her illness. Even Alex's family didn't know until afterward. It was worth all the trouble to know that my little girl was happy the last year of her life."

I could see that Mrs. Lavelle thought of life in terms of the soap operas she watched. And he was still supporting her mother, even providing television to keep her from being bored. Somehow, it didn't seem quite fair to him.

"Alex was crazy about Elizabeth," Mrs. Lavelle said. "He had the very best doctors. And he was always bringing her little surprises—new nightgowns, stuffed animals, anything he thought she would fancy. He just couldn't do enough for her.

"Alex is a good man; I don't care what anybody says," the old lady said. "He told me today he would go on sending the money just the same, even though he was getting married again." There was a note of defiance in her voice. She did not look at me but smoothed the print dress over her knees, tracing its pattern with her finger.

The younger woman coughed, looked at me, and said, "His new wife will have something to say about that, Mamma."

"No, I—that is, I'll be glad for Alex to go on helping you."

Both of them looked relieved. I saw that the daughter was going to thank me, but before she could speak, I said, "Mrs. Lavelle, did Elizabeth ever have anything wrong with her besides the leukemia? An injury perhaps that left a scar?"

She stared at me. "Why, no. There wasn't a blemish on her skin anywhere. Why do you ask?"

"Myra thought she had one."

"That sounds like something Myra would say," Mrs. Lavelle said. "She never liked Elizabeth."

"Now, Mamma—"

"You know it's the truth. She treated her like dirt, like she didn't belong at Wisteria. 'You're the boss here,' I used to tell Elizabeth. 'All you've got to do is tell Alex to make Roy and Myra move out.' But Elizabeth was too kind for her own good. She wouldn't do it."

She paused and then said in an aggrieved voice, "Myra had the nerve to try to keep Elizabeth's bedroom suite after she died. Said Alex had paid for it and she had picked it out, so it belonged at Wisteria. But I told her it was bought for Elizabeth, and I meant to have it. Alex wanted me to have it, of course. He talked pretty rough to Myra. 'For God's sake let her have it,' he said. 'I never want to see it again anyway.' He couldn't stand to look at any of Elizabeth's things after she died."

Chapter 14

I was humming as I started the car. Now I would not have to bother Dr. Manning. I felt as if I had come out of a dark alley into a cheerful daylit street where people were moving about in ordinary everyday pursuits. Myra's dark hints were blown away. They were lies. Of course she knew the cause of Elizabeth's death. She had wanted to make me doubt Alex. But even Myra's hate did not matter now that I knew the truth. Elizabeth's death was tragic, but there was nothing sinister or unnatural about it. Alex was guilty of nothing. "He is a good man," Mrs. Lavelle had said, "and I don't care what anybody says."

Why did she put it that way? Was there gossip about Alex?

It was another financial burden added to the ones I already knew about. No wonder Alex hadn't remarried before. I didn't see how he could manage all the responsibility he already carried. Of course his marrying me wouldn't add any financial burden. Might even be a help to him.

When I drove into the driveway at Wisteria, I saw the crowd at the pool. I hurried upstairs to change. But first I took my wedding dress out of the big box, careful to smooth out all the folds. Touching the pearly smoothness of the fabric brought back my gloomy feeling that perhaps I was not destined to wear this dress. But that was foolish. I would wear the dress; perhaps I would even wear it Sunday, as I had planned.

Alex left the pool and came across the lawn to meet me. "You're late," he said. "I was worried about you."

"I thought I told you I had some errands to do today. They took longer than I expected."

"How's the new car?"

"Come see."

He looked at it carefully inside and out and raised the hood to look at the engine. "You can have my garage space," he said. I started to protest, and he raised his hand. "No, don't argue. We always put the newest cars in the garage. It's a family rule. I'll park outside; there's plenty of room."

"Alex, I saw you in the city," I said.

"You did? Where?"

"Coming out of town toward the highway. I followed you because I thought you were taking a shortcut."

"Why didn't you toot your horn and let me know you were behind?" His voice was careless, but he was watching me closely. It reminded me of the furtive way he had looked around before entering Mrs. Lavelle's house. Suddenly I wasn't sure I wanted to tell him about my visit to her.

"I was going to signal, but—" I stared at him helplessly. I couldn't think of an excuse to give. I wished I hadn't mentioned this. He would know I had spied on him.

"You saw me stop, is that it? And now you want to know whom I saw. Well, I'm not going to tell you."

I was astonished at his vehemence. "Why not?"

"It would only cause another quarrel. It's my business. It has nothing to do with you."

"You keep saying that, Alex. You're trying to keep your life separate from mine. That isn't what marriage means."

"We aren't married yet."

"No, and it begins to look as if we never will be, unless you can share your life with me." I felt as if I were replaying an old record. We had said the same words many times before. I was weary of them, hopeless of ever making Alex see that I only wanted to help him push away the past, which was blocking our marriage.

He turned away from me and kicked absently at the tires on my car. "If it means so much, I'll tell you who I saw." His voice was reluctant, and he didn't look at me.

I said wearily, "You don't have to. I went to see her myself after you left."

He whirled around to face me accusingly. "You followed me. Good God, do you distrust me that much?"

"Alex, I'm sorry, but being in love with you doesn't make a complete idiot of me. Things have to make sense even if I am in love. I can face danger, but I want to understand what I'm up against. It seems to have something to do with your first marriage, but you won't talk about that."

He turned away while I was speaking. He stood looking toward the distant trees, refusing to let me see his face. "I've tried to forget my first marriage," he said. "I'm a different man now, at least I hope I am. I thought we would be happy. I could see us together here at Wisteria, watching our children grow up, growing old together. It would be as if I had never been married to anyone else."

"Mrs. Lavelle said you never got over Elizabeth's death," I said slowly. "She was right, wasn't she?"

He looked as if he hated me. "Good God, no," he said violently. "Can't you understand anything? There was nothing to get over. I was glad when she was dead. Glad. Does that shock you? Now you see why I don't want to talk about her, why I'd like to forget we were ever married. I hated her, and I was glad when she died."

I didn't think of what he had just said. Odd, disconnected little impressions filled my mind: the buzzing of voices from the swimming pool, a muscle jumping in Alex's jaw, a car going by on the road. I thought how inappropriate it seemed to be dressed in swim suits for what might be the most important talk of our lives.

Alex paced up and down on the driveway, the rubber soles of his bath shoes making no sound. "Have you any idea what it's like to live with an invalid?" he asked. "The complaints, the demands, the petulant recriminations. The harrassing necessity of doing twice as much work to meet the bills and having only half as much time to do it in because she expects you to spend every minute with her. The feeling of being hemmed in, having not even a moment to call your own. The disgusting physical aspects of illness—bedpans and transfusions and injections. I was young and healthy; I'd never had any experience with sickness. It was all horrible to me."

His words were pouring out in a turbulent stream, spilling over each other. "I told myself it was a thousand times worse for her; I tried to be patient and understanding. I spent a lot of time with her. Oh, the crushing boredom of those hours. Listening to how she felt, what the doctors said, who had been to see her and what they said."

He stopped his agitated pacing and kicked at a rock. He did not look at me. "Then she would have a remission; the disease would lie dormant for a little while, and she could be up and about. But I felt no different toward her then. We had nothing in common. She was like a child, playing with her dog, dressing up for parties, begging for new dresses and jewelry. She didn't love me. She was too selfish to love anyone. You saw her mother; you should be able to imagine what Elizabeth was like."

He looked at me, his dark face turgid with emotion. "You thought we made some strange pact on our wedding night. God, if you only knew . . ." He stopped. I thought he was not going to say any more. But after a minute he resumed.

"It was shameful and degrading; you were right about that. But not in the way you thought. There was no pact, no promise." His mouth twisted. "In fact, no wedding night. I'll spare you the details. But I never touched her. She didn't want a husband. She wanted someone who would give her pretty things and entertain her and never, never make any demands."

Throughout his agitated recital I had remained silent, shocked beyond speech. Now he had stopped talking, but I felt numb. His impassioned words beating against me had driven out all feeling. I was conscious of everything, but I felt nothing. I had lived his torment; now I was insensate.

Alex was standing very still, watching me. His emotions seemed gone now. His face was pale and empty. After a moment he shrugged. "Now you know why I feel guilty about Elizabeth," he said. "I didn't want to tell you. I didn't want you to know I was the kind of man who could hate a sick girl. She couldn't help being sick. Perhaps she couldn't help being dull and boring and selfish. God, who am I to talk about anyone else being selfish!"

Feeling came back to me. I ran to Alex, took his

arm. I knew what I would say to him. Look at me, Alex. I love you. I love you more than ever now. You've no reason to feel guilty. It wasn't your fault; you couldn't help the way you felt. You did your best. You were good to her. Mrs. Lavelle said so. You must forget it, never let it trouble you again. We'll be happy, you'll see. Jumbled words, not well organized, but Alex would know what I meant.

But before I could say them a cool voice behind me said, "So this is the new car."

I turned, and it was Myra. She hadn't been in the pool yet. She was wearing a sky blue bikini which somehow managed to suggest a bedroom rather than a swimming pool. Alex was staring at her with blind eyes. I chattered about the car to give him a chance to collect himself. "I bought it today from Mr. Burney. I started to get a blue Buick like Alex's, but then I saw this one and liked the color."

"It does rather hit one in the eye," she said. "I prefer something less gaudy for myself . . . Alex, can't you do something about Britt? He has disappeared with Merry Gordon again, and Cal if looking for her. I'm afraid there'll be trouble."

"I'll see if I can find them," Alex said. "Come on, Tracy, you can help me hunt."

"You go ahead," Myra said. "I want Tracy to meet the Petersons. They are just back from Europe," she said to me as Alex walked ahead, "and that's all Evelyn will talk about. They saw London and Paris and Rome, although I daresay they didn't get off the beaten tourist track." Underneath her tone of contempt I thought I detected a note of envy.

I listened to Mrs. Peterson's travelogue and another lady's account of her operation and a detailing of the educational difficulties of someone's son. I tried to watch for Alex. I wanted to finish our interrupted conversation. I must tell him I understood about Elizabeth.

Finally he came back, but, preoccupied with the problem of Britt, he seemed to have forgotten what we were talking about earlier. "They were in the garden," he said. "Britt was angry when I interrupted. I doubt if he'll come back to the pool, and it's just as well. Cal has a terrible temper, and that little fool Merry is as likely as not to tell him where she was.... Are you ready to swim?"

I looked at the ruffled water, blue at the edges and shading to chartreuse and gold where the sunshine made a path across it. For all its beauty, it suddenly looked treacherous, menacing. I was afraid of its cold depths. In my imagination I could feel the shock of going under, the pain of being unable to breathe. I couldn't go in.

"Don't forget now, you're to stay with me," Alex said.

At the sound of his voice I shook off my foreboding. Alex would protect me. Nothing could happen this time.

I realized later that something *was* happening at that very moment. But I didn't know about it until I got back to my room and found my wedding dress on the floor.

Chapter 15

I recognized the dress immediately. Even lying in a tattered heap on the floor, the satin gleamed with a pearly luster. With a cry I rushed to pick it up. Long jagged pieces of satin fluttered to the floor. Some of them were smudged with black. The dress had been hacked to ribbons and the fabric piled up and trampled by dirty feet. Tears of helpless rage filled my eyes. I scooped up the remaining pieces and went down the hall to Alex's room.

"Just a minute," he called and then came to the door buttoning his shirt. He stared at the material in my arms. "What is it?"

"My wedding dress. When I got back to my room, I found it like this." I held up the pieces.

He looked at them dumbly. "How vicious!" he finally said.

"I'm frightened, Alex. It's as if whoever did this wanted to do it to me."

He shook his head. "No, I don't think so. Your other clothes weren't touched? Only the wedding dress. It's the same as before. Someone is trying to prevent our wedding. He must have thought we were going ahead in spite of everything. So he tore up your dress."

"But who?"

"I have no idea."

We were silent. "Anyone could have done it," I said at length. I thought of the crowd at the pool watching me go in with the big box. I thought of Britt slipping out of Myra's room. I thought of Myra with her lies about Elizabeth. And I thought of the ghost threatening me. "It was a woman," I said. "It's something a woman would think of doing."

He looked at me sharply. "I thought I convinced you there is no other woman in my life."

There was one, but neither of us mentioned her. The villainous destruction of my dress became understandable when I remembered her. There had been no pact Alex said. She had not even been his wife, not truly. But he had also said she was selfish and demanding. She did not want Alex to be happy. . . . Oh, what difference did the reason she haunted me make? I *felt* her malevolent presence.

We had been standing in the hall outside Alex's room for some minutes. He looked at his watch. "You should get dressed. We'll have to leave soon."

"Grandfather!" I cried. "I almost forgot." I pushed the pieces of the wedding dress into his hands and ran to my room.

I saw Grandfather the minute he came through the door of the plane. "There he is," I said to Alex. "The tall man in gray with the mustache."

"That's your *grandfather*?" Alex asked.

"He looks quite young, doesn't he? It's because he is so straight and hasn't lost his hair."

I ran to greet him and brought him to Alex. They spoke politely, with the wariness of two men who love the same woman. Grandfather's voice, always faintly British, was very clipped, a sure sign he hadn't yet given his approval of Alex.

"It's good to have you here, Grandfather," I said, giving his arm a squeeze.

As Alex left to get the luggage I turned to Grandfather. "Well, what do you think of him?"

Grandfather's sharp blue eyes followed Alex's retreating figure. "It's too soon to tell," he said. "Doesn't matter anyway. It's what you think of him that counts." He looked down at me. "You're thinner, and you look as if you haven't been sleeping well."

"You should know by now that women like to be thin. I'm fine. Honestly."

We talked casually on the way home. Alex seemed interested in Grandfather's travels, and Grandfather had the knack of telling brief amusing anecdotes. I found myself laughing heartily for the first time in weeks. Alex laughed, too, and for a moment I was startled. It seemed a long time since

I had heard that sound. It was good to have Grandfather here. I felt lighthearted again.

It was after dinner that the subject of the wills came up. Alex and I had taken Grandfather on a tour of the house and ended up in the living room. Myra and Britt were there, Britt reading the afternoon paper and Myra knitting something blue, her needles clicking rapidly and efficiently.

"It's a beautiful house," Grandfather said to Myra. "Are you a trained decorator?"

She flushed with pleasure. "No, but I studied a lot about the various periods and styles while I was doing it. I thought everything turned out rather well."

"I'm eager to see the grounds, too," Grandfather said.

"They're rather run down, I'm afraid," Alex said. "I've been so busy building up the farm that I haven't had the time or the money for landscaping. But Tracy wants to spend her own money to restore the garden."

Britt looked up. "She'll probably change her mind when she finds out about labor costs. It would take a fortune to put that garden back in shape."

"I don't care what it costs," I said. "My heart is set on doing it, and Jim is going to help me. Jim Cantwell, Alex's partner," I said to Grandfather.

"I didn't know you had a partner," Grandfather said to Alex. He added in his brisk, precise voice, "However, that doesn't matter since I would prefer Tracy's money to be managed separately from yours. My concern, naturally, is for her protection."

Britt's blue eyes rounded in surprise. He looked at Grandfather and then at me. The surprise disappeared; it was as if a shutter had been closed, hiding what was going on inside. Myra dropped her knitting and left it lying on the floor unnoticed. Grandfather didn't know, of course, that they were unaware of my money. They must have been shocked by his statement. It sounded as if he wanted to secure Alex's property for me. They were thinking Grandfather crafty and grasping.

"Grandfather, that has all been taken care of," I said hurriedly. "Alex and I made our will last week."

"Wills? What kind of wills?"

"Why, he left everything to me, and I left everything to him."

He stared at me and then turned to look at Alex. Alex seemed embarrassed. He said, "I didn't know then that Tracy had money to leave anyone. That is, I thought perhaps a few hundred dollars—but I never dreamed she had nearly half a million."

I didn't know whether it was Britt or Myra who gasped. When I looked around, they were both motionless, listening intently.

"It will be considerably more than that when I'm gone," Grandfather said. "Tracy is my only heir . . . But why would you make wills before you are married?"

"It's something one is inclined to put off," Alex said. "I wanted to get it over with and be sure Tracy was protected. As I said, I had no idea she was a rich girl. When she insisted on making a will, too, I thought I was indulging a whim."

"I still don't see—even without a will, wouldn't everything go to Tracy once you were married?"

"No, this will supercedes a previous one in which Britt and Pam were my heirs."

"But why do it before the wedding? What if something had happened before you married?"

"I wanted Tracy to have my property," Alex said stubbornly. "I have no close relatives except Britt and Pam, and they no longer need anything from me. If anything happened, I wanted Tracy to have it."

"It seems to me that you were hasty," Grandfather said. "However, it's done now." He turned to Myra. "I apologize for talking business my first night here, but it seemed best since the wedding is tomorrow."

Myra glanced at me and raised her eyebrows. I shook my head, hoping she would understand that I hadn't told Grandfather the wedding was off. Apparently she guessed my meaning, because she rolled up her yarn and said, "I'm a little tired, so I think I'll go up now."

Grandfather said he was tired too and would see us in the morning.

"I didn't forget your buttermilk, Grandfather," I said. "I bought some today. I'll bring it up to your room."

But when I came into the hall with the tray, Britt was just starting upstairs. "I'll take it up, Tracy. I'm going now anyway. You get back to Alex. You two have little enough time together."

I was touched by his consideration. I did want very badly to talk to Alex. I hadn't yet had a chance to tell him I understood his feelings toward Elizabeth. I thought, too, that Grandfather's criticism of our business arrangements might have left some ruffled feelings. I gave the tray to Britt and went back to the living room.

The first thing Alex said was, "Tracy, your grandfather doesn't like me."

"There hasn't been time, Alex. He doesn't dislike you, and Grandfather doesn't warm up to people right away. I suppose he's too hardheaded a businessman to trust anyone at first sight."

"I believe your grandfather thinks I'm marrying you for your money."

"No, he doesn't think that. I'm sure he understands."

But I wasn't sure he did. I wasn't sure I did myself. What Alex said sounded so reasonable. It *was* reasonable; it was all just as Alex said. So why couldn't I rid myself of those traitorous thoughts? Why did I keep remembering that I had been pursued by danger ever since I came here, that someone had tried to kill me, that only Alex would profit by my death?

Alex said, "He still thinks the wedding is tomorrow. We'll have to give him some excuse."

"It won't be easy to do. Grandfather isn't easy to fool. However, I can say my wedding dress isn't ready, which is certainly true enough."

"I'm sorry about all this, Tracy. But it will be cleared up soon, and we can marry without putting you in any more danger. That is, if you still want to marry me after all I told you today."

"Oh, Alex, I do." When Alex was holding me in his arms like this, everything seemed all right, and I believed in our future.

I went up to bed feeling better, more hopeful. It was only after I lay down that I suddenly realized Grandfather might be having doubts of his own. But if he knew the whole story, he would realize that Alex loved me, that my money had nothing to do with it. I wanted Grandfather to like Alex, not tolerate him for my sake, but really like him.

I got up and put on the pink robe lying at the foot of the bed. Sticking my feet into pink satin slides, I started down the hall to Grandfather's room. As I expected, there was a light under the door. I knocked lightly.

No one answered. I knocked again a little louder. Still no answer. I was puzzled. Grandfather had never seemed hard of hearing. I'd thought all his faculties were as keen as they had ever been. I opened the door and looked in. Grandfather was in bed; he had dropped off to sleep while reading, leaving his light on. The book had slid out of his hand and lay on the bedcovers. I thought how different people looked asleep, how strange. Grandfather's face was in repose; none of his customary expression played across it.

Was his face too white? The way he was lying, in an uncomfortable sideways position, didn't look natural. My heart plummeted in sudden fright. I ran to the bed. "Grandfather?" I cried.

He didn't answer. My heart was pounding in

panic. I put my hand on his chest and felt a great wave of thankfulness. He was breathing, and his heart was beating. But too faintly, I thought worriedly, as if it might stop any time. I shook him, but he didn't open his eyes. He was like an empty stocking, limp and floppy.

My panic returned. I ran into the hall, pounded on Alex's door. Not waiting for him to open it, I cried, "Alex, something has happened to Grandfather. You'd better get a doctor right away."

In my fright I didn't even remember we had a doctor in the house until I saw Chris come out, struggling into a robe. "What's the trouble?" he asked.

"Grandfather. He's in some kind of coma."

Chris was right behind me as I went into the room. He crossed swiftly to the bed and bent over. "Get my bag, Alex. You know where it is. Tracy, tell Pam to call the hospital and tell them I'm bringing him in. Then wake Myra and send her in here." He looked around. "Where's Britt? He can help us get him to the car."

"Here I am," Britt said. "What's wrong? Heart?"

I didn't know what Chris answered; I was already down the hall calling Pam and Myra.

Time lost its normal rhythm. Everyone was hurrying, running about, shouting questions. Yet in spite of all the bustle, it seemed to take far too long for them to get Grandfather to the car. The minutes crawled. I was frantically impatient. Why didn't they leave? What were they waiting for? At last they sped down the driveway. Britt was driving with Alex beside him and Chris with Grandfather on the back seat. I raced upstairs to jump into some clothes and follow them.

Myra was already dressed and had her car keys in her hand. "I'll drive you, Tracy," she said. "You've no business driving in the state you're in. Don't worry. He's going to be all right. I feel that very strongly, and you must believe it, too."

Myra's confidence bolstered my own wavering faith, and I felt better. With the part of my mind that wasn't scared to death, I realized that Myra was being kinder to me now than at any time since I'd been here.

Chapter 16

At eight o'clock the next morning, I was on my way back to the hospital. We hadn't got home until two, so I'd had only a few hours sleep, but I wasn't conscious of being tired. I felt alert, and the world seemed bright. Grandfather was going to be all right. He had taken an overdose of sleeping pills, but fortunately I had found him in time.

I went to his room and stood looking at him. Lying in bed with the wrinkles smoothed out of his face, he looked younger, almost like a little boy, vulnerable and defenseless. What a frail hold we have on life, I thought.

I said as much to Chris when I sat in his office.

He shook his head. "Grandfather's action was more than a simple mistake," he said. "You'll need to know that, Tracy, in order to take proper precautions. Either he is so forgetful he took his medicine about six times, or he did it deliberately."

"That's impossible. Grandfather is reluctant to take medicine of any kind. He believes in natural remedies. I doubt if he even takes sleeping pills. If he does, I'm sure he's careful of the dosage."

"Has he been depressed lately?"

"I haven't been with him for several months until last night, but he seemed relatively happy."

"We'll know more after we talk with him."

The question loomed black and frightening in my mind: Had someone tried to kill Grandfather?

When I walked into the living room at Mrs. St. John's, I was conscious of a sudden silence, the kind of silence that falls sometimes when the object of a piece of juicy gossip comes on the scene. Then everyone started talking again, asking about Grandfather and expressing their regrets.

"I've often thought how easy it would be for such an accident to happen," Mrs. St. John said. "When something becomes so automatic, it's hard to remember whether you've done it that day. I frequently go back two or three times to lock my doors at night. I should think it would be the same with taking pills."

"Yes, we think that's how it happened," I said. I realized that to keep down gossip, I was being less than honest. Only a few days ago when Alex and I argued about my lunch with Jim I called him cowardly for doing the same thing. Perhaps, as Jim said, compromise was a part of growing up.

Mrs. St. John handed out paper and pencils. We

unscrambled letters to make words like proposal and promise and engagement. We filled in blanks with the names of vegetables: Do you *carrot* all for me? *Lettuce* be married. Then I opened my gifts. It was a miscellaneous shower, and I got all sorts of things—linens, kitchen gadgets, lingerie. Althea Jones gave me a flat plexiglass paperweight containing a small photograph of Wisteria.

"How clever!" I said. "You must have made this yourself."

"Yes." She looked embarrassed. "I'm sorry about the inscription. It's an old Irish saying. I guess it isn't very amusing after what happened."

"From ghoulies and ghosties and long-legged beasties, and things that go bump in the night, good Lord, deliver us," I read.

For a moment I couldn't think of anything to say. Then I laughed. "Thanks, Althea. Maybe this will be a talisman."

I hadn't realized anyone outside the family knew about the ghost. My eyes went to Myra's face, and by its guileless look I guessed she had told them. With an indulgent smile for my folly, no doubt.

Pam had come with Myra, but she offered to help me load my gifts and ride home with me. When she put the paperweight in, she said, "Althea was embarrassed about this. She made it before she knew about the ghost."

"Then Myra must have told the story today."

"Yes, just before you came. She meant it as a joke," Pam said apologetically, "but I wish she hadn't told it. Some of those women are more malicious than Myra. Mrs. St. John, for instance."

"What did she say?"

"That chasing ghosts could serve as an excuse for other things. I asked her what she meant. She saw I was angry and wouldn't say any more. But later she told about seeing you and Jim lunching together. I started to deny it, but Myra cut me off. 'I'm afraid it's true,' she said, 'but Tracy meant no harm. She has been brought up differently, and it will take time for her to learn our customs.'"

I could imagine Myra saying just that, intimating something wrong with my relationship with Jim but in an excusing way so that everyone, even Pam, would think her loyal.

Alex offered to go to the hospital with me in the afternoon, but I refused. I wanted to go alone to talk to Grandfather about the accident. Grandfather wouldn't admit his forgetfulness before Alex, but I didn't think he would mind telling me.

But I was mistaken. The first thing he said to me was, "Well, I'm still alive." And the second was, "Who tried to kill me last night?"

"What makes you ask that?"

"Because I damn well didn't take those sleeping pills myself. I have some; got them last fall when I had trouble with my back, and I take them once in a while when it flares up again. But I didn't take any last night."

"Are you sure, Grandfather?"

"Of course I'm sure."

"Anyone can make a mistake."

"I didn't. I told the sheriff that a few minutes ago. Someone else gave me those pills, and it isn't hard to know how. They were in the buttermilk. I wouldn't have noticed the taste; the stuff is so foul anyhow."

"I thought you liked it."

"Good Lord, no. I drink it because I read somewhere that it's good for the digestion."

"Grandfather, I can't believe the milk was drugged. I poured it for you myself."

"Was the carton open? It had been thrown away by the time the sheriff got there."

"I opened it. I wanted to taste it and see if I could tell why you seemed to like it so much."

"Then anyone in the house could have drugged it," he said. "I suppose they knew it was for me?"

"Yes. Myra asked who it was for when I brought it in. She said no one at Wisteria drinks it."

"But why would any one of them want to kill me?"

I shook my head. "I don't know, Grandfather." Perhaps there doesn't have to be any reason for evil, I thought. Perhaps it lives in certain houses and takes in all that comes within its reach. Was that the answer? Was there a brooding malevolence built into the house itself?

Grandfather must have seen something in my face. He said urgently, "Tracy, I don't want you to stay at Wisteria any longer."

"But Grandfather, I'm going to marry Alex. I'll live there the rest of my life."

"Not until I can get out of here and get to the bottom of this," he said. "There are a lot of things I don't like at Wisteria. That sister-in-law watches you like a spider looking at a fly. Also, I still have a few questions to ask Alex. It seems to me he was in a big hurry to get those wills made. People don't think about dying when they are in love."

"His first wife died very young. Perhaps that made him more conscious of what might happen." But I couldn't blame Grandfather for his doubts. I'd had some of the same thoughts.

"Even the house—it's pretty enough, but there's a cold feeling to it. It's too perfect."

Now that Grandfather mentioned it, I knew he was right. It was one of the things that bothered me. I felt the house was so perfect I couldn't touch it. That was why I had decided to restore the garden.

"Tracy, they say I'll be out of here tomorrow, so promise me you'll move out at least for tonight. There must be a hotel in town."

"Yes. But I couldn't do that to Alex and his family. It would look as if I suspected them of trying to kill me."

"You?" Grandfather's voice rose. "What do you mean? Has something else happened? Something *has* happened, something you haven't told me about."

"No, nothing since last night."

"You think the sleeping pills were meant for you instead of me? You must have meant something. Tell me, Tracy."

He looked too excited. I must calm him. But Grandfather was too shrewd to fool. I would have to tell him part of the truth. So I said, "There have been some other incidents. My cameo has been stolen, and my wedding dress was cut up. I wonder if someone isn't trying to prevent my marriage."

"Then you must let them think they've succeeded."

"But we would never find out who it was and why. I would always be frightened. No, Grandfather. We must catch whoever it is. I'll be careful."

"Tracy, you don't realize the risk. I can't let you take it. If you're going to stay, then at least I'll be there to protect you. My eyes aren't blinded by love. I'll see more than you do. Now get out of here and let me get dressed."

"You can't leave, Grandfather. Chris said you were to stay until tomorrow."

"Chris be hanged. Maybe he's in it himself; maybe that's why he wants me out of the way. If you're going to spend the night at Wisteria, then so am I." He started to get up.

"No, wait," I cried. "All right, I'll go to a hotel if that will satisfy you."

Chapter 17

I walked out of the air-conditioned hospital into a stream bath. It was too hot, too oppressive. There was a sense of waiting in the atmosphere, a feeling that this heat must explode in violence.

Sandra was coming out the front door when I got to Wisteria. I had forgotten she was back. Her long plain face looked sympathetic as she asked, "How is your grandfather, Tracy?"

"Much better, thanks. He's going to be all right and can leave the hospital tomorrow, Chris says."

"It was a terrible thing to happen, but you were lucky it was no worse."

"Yes. If it hadn't been for my going to his room, and Chris's being a doctor, and Britt's getting him to the hospital so fast, he would have died. Everyone helped. They were all wonderful."

"Britt said it was an accident, that he apparently forgot he had already taken his usual dose."

There was no question in her voice, and yet I had a feeling it was a question and that she was waiting tensely for my answer.

"It's hard to know how things happen," I said cautiously. "One gets so in the habit of things. Grandfather doesn't remember taking any pills at all last night."

Her face paled. She looked at the wisteria across the side fence. When her eyes came back to me, they were troubled. "Tracy, Britt told me about your cameo and the ghost. I'm worried about you. That time you almost drowned—maybe it wasn't an accident. And now your grandfather—it looks as if someone is trying to harm both of you."

"The thought has crossed my mind," I said dryly.

Sandra shivered. "There's something about this place. I've never liked it. There have been too many tragedies—Elizabeth's death and Roy's accident—"

"Accident? I thought he died with a heart attack or something."

"No, he missed the curve on the other side of the creek and went into the water. He was trapped under the car and drowned. They didn't find him until the next day."

"But they were sure it was an accident?"

"Oh, of course. I didn't mean that. He was drunk; several witnesses said that. No, there was no foul play. But it's strange all the same that so many tragedies happen to the people who live here. It's as if the house was—doomed. Tracy, I'm worried. I wish you would go away from here before something else happens."

"It's queer you should say that, Sandra, because it's what I've decided to do temporarily."

"Would you like to stay with us? There's plenty of room, and Mother would be glad to have you."

"Why, thank you. I'd planned to go to a hotel, and I was dreading the talk it would cause. But no one will think it strange if I visit you. It's a perfect solution."

"Can I help you pack?"

"No, I want to talk to Alex first."

All her worry seemed to have disappeared, and she was her old self as she said, "I hope you have better luck talking with Alex than I did with Britt. He walked out on me, saying he had to go to the store. Men are the devil, aren't they? . . . I'm going home. Just come when you're ready."

I found Alex in his office. "I'm finished, come on in," he said. "How was your grandfather?"

"Fine. He'll be able to leave tomorrow."

"Does he know how it happened?"

"He thinks someone tried to kill him."

After a moment of silence, he said, "Why?"

I shrugged. "He can't imagine."

"And you? What do you think?"

"I don't know, Alex. I just don't know. It's so senseless. Why would anyone want to kill Grandfather? If it had been me—" I paused.

"Yes. Go on."

179

"Someone does want to kill me—or at least to prevent my marriage to you. I've already faced that. Someone or something. I don't know why. I've thought and thought. There are a lot of reasons for murder, I suppose—fear, jealousy, money, a lot of others. Perhaps if I understood all of you better, I'd know why."

"I don't know why anyone would fear you. There's no one to be jealous, since I've never been in love with anyone else. So that leaves money." He was watching me narrowly, but I refused to meet his eyes. I remained miserably silent. What could I say? I didn't suspect Alex. Of course I didn't. But I had protested too many times, apologized too often for things I wasn't guilty of.

The silence stretched out, became uncomfortable. Suddenly I realized it was not only in the room but in the whole house. All the small noises—voices, footsteps, music from radios or record players—were missing. "Where is everybody?" I asked.

"Chris hasn't come in, and Britt went back to the store, I think. Pam and Myra are looking at the house again."

"Perhaps it's just as well they aren't here. You can tell them I've gone to spend the night with Sandra."

"Wasn't that a sudden decision? You didn't mention it before."

"Grandfather insisted that I leave Wisteria," I said frankly. "I think he would have left the hospital this afternoon if I hadn't promised."

He looked at me silently, and then his eyes

moved to a picture on the wall behind my head. "I see," he said.

I wanted to say, It has nothing to do with you, Alex. If he had looked at me, if he had made any move, I could have said something, but he kept staring at the picture, not saying anything.

I turned and left. The stairs creaked as I walked up, and the ticking of the grandfather clock in the upper hall sounded loud and lonesome. Something in the silence made me uneasy.

I hurried into my room and closed the door, pushing the button to lock it. Then I packed hurriedly, taking only what I needed tonight and tomorrow morning. I was not leaving Wisteria for good. I would do what I promised Grandfather, but I would be back tomorrow.

I opened the door of my room and peered cautiously into the hall, half expecting to see a ghostly white figure. But there was nothing except the silence, like a threatening unseen presence. I scurried downstairs and, unwilling to stay in the house any longer than I had to, took the nearest door out, the one at the end of the hall to the terrace. But even outside I did not feel safe.

It was almost twilight, and clouds added to the darkness. I could still see, but just barely. I reached the garage, set my bag down on the concrete floor, and fumbled in my purse for the car keys. My hands touched an envelope, a compact, a package of mints, but no car keys. Desperately I felt again. They must be there. Then I remembered. They were in my hand when I went into Alex's office. I must have put them down there.

How annoying! I had taken my leave of Alex, and I didn't want to go back. Besides, I was reluctant to cross the dark yard and enter the still, silent house.

Then I remembered that I had a magnetized box like Alex's for my extra key. It was Ed Burney's customary gift to the purchaser of a new car. I clicked on the garage light and went to the front of the car. It took me a few minutes to figure out how to raise the hood, but finally I had it. My hands closed on the little box—

And then the light went out. Slowly. Gradually darkening while sparkles of blue and gold and vermillion danced in front of my eyes. My head hurt and I was falling—

Why, someone hit me, I thought in sudden terror.

When I came to, I was lying outside. Dew was damp on my back, and the grass blades prickled my legs. It was very dark; the stars were obscured by clouds. A black shape moved beside me. I jumped and cried out.

Jim's voice answered me. "You're all right," he said. "She's coming to," he called, turning his head toward the sound of running footsteps.

In another moment Alex pounded up. "What's wrong? What happened?" he cried. He sounded as if he couldn't breathe.

"She was lying on the garage floor with the engine running."

"I'm all right. Help me up, please." My voice sounded hoarse. I cleared my throat. I felt dizzy and my head jarred achingly with every step, but other than that I seemed to be all right. Still, they insisted on supporting me to Alex's office where I lay down on the sofa.

Alex turned to Jim. "How did you happen to find her?"

"I was sitting in the garden thinking about how to fix the sundial when I heard the sound of a car engine in the garage. At first I didn't pay much attention. It took a few minutes for it to get through to me that the car was idling far too long. I went to see why and found the doors locked. Then I knew something must be wrong, so I broke in. Pried the padlock off the side door with the pruning shears."

"Where did you find Tracy?"

"Crumpled on the floor in front of the car."

"Someone hit me," I said. "I looked under the hood to get the extra key, and just as I started to raise my head up, someone hit me."

"Who?"

"I don't know."

Chris came in then and, after examining me, agreed that I was all right. All I had was a small lump on my head. Just as he finished, Britt came down the hall to the open door of the office and said, "What's going on?"

"Tracy has been hurt."

"Hurt?"

"Jim found her in the garage, knocked out."

His eyes looked puzzled, and he seemed unable to do anything except parrot the words he heard. "Knocked out?"

"She was lying on the floor. Someone hit her on

the head while she was getting her key from under the hood."

"That sounds fantastic." Britt seemed to be puzzling over the problem, trying to figure out what happened. "Could she have hit her head on the hood when she raised up? Or maybe it fell on her. Was it up or down?"

Alex looked at Jim. "Down," Jim said.

"The contusion could have been caused by the car hood or even the concrete floor," Chris said.

Alex looked at me. I said slowly, "I don't think the hood fell. The garage lights were on. Wouldn't I have seen it coming down?"

"Wait a minute," Alex said. "The doors were closed. Who locked them and started the car engine?"

Britt said gently, "Tracy, did you do it yourself? We know you've been troubled, but—"

It took a moment for me to understand what he was saying. "Why, you think I tried to kill myself!" I said.

No one spoke. I looked from one face to another, but they looked doubtful and puzzled. I was angry. "The things that have happened to me since I came here are enough to make anyone contemplate suicide if he's the type. But I'm not. You can believe that or not just as you please."

I got up from the sofa. I would go to Sandra's immediately. But I was dizzy. Someone would have to take me to Sandra's. Who? I looked around, realizing that I did not trust any of them. Not even Alex. I didn't feel like going to Sandra's now. All I wanted was to lie down somewhere in the quiet dark. "Somebody can call Sandra and tell her I don't feel like coming tonight," I said. "I'm going up to my room. I'm going to lock myself in, and if anyone comes, I'm going to shoot that gun Alex gave me without asking any questions."

Their faces were blank with shock as I left the room, not looking back. I locked my door, kicked off my shoes, and lay down across the bed. Someone had almost killed me, and nobody believed it. Not even Alex. And after everything else that had happened, he should know—

After everything else. But that was it. That was why they thought I might have tried to kill myself. They were looking back at the other events and seeing in them the preliminaries to suicide. They were seeing what happened tonight not as the culmination of my own unbalanced thoughts and actions.

I was wrong in thinking someone wanted to drown me. There was only one reason for everything that happened, and that reason was to make me behave in such a way that when I finally died, apparently by my own hand, everyone would believe I had been insane. Suicide while of unsound mind; that was how the newspapers always put it.

They would blame Grandfather, and he might even wonder himself if he had neglected me.

And they would probably even accuse me of trying to kill Grandfather!

The only reason none of it happened was that Jim happened to be in the garden and heard the car engine.

But Alex was in his office. Why did he not hear?

How did the murderer dare try to kill me with Alex's windows overlooking the garage and Alex in the office? Had the murderer not known Alex was there?

Alex was alone in his office. He would have heard me come down the stairs and turn toward the back door. From his window he could have seen me go into the garage.

Not Alex.

When I told him I was leaving, he said, "I see," in that cool voice. He did not look at me.

He wanted to marry me. We would have children, he said, and grow old together. But he kept postponing our wedding.

Not Alex.

I jerked to a sitting position, and my head throbbed worse. More gently I slid to the edge of my bed and stepped into my shoes. I walked slowly and carefully, trying to keep from jarring the hammers in my head. I had to talk to Alex. I wanted to hear him say he did not know I was in the garage until he heard Jim's shout.

His office door was standing open, but no one was inside. I moved to the window and looked out. They were all at the garage—Alex, Jim, Britt, Chris—even Pam and Myra had joined them. I knew the sheriff was there, too, for his car was standing in the driveway. No doubt he would want to talk to me when he finished examining the scene. I would wait here until they finished and came in. I sat down in the nearest chair, the one at Alex's desk. Dully my eyes rested on the framed snapshot of myself. My smiling face looked childish and silly. When could I ever have been so light-hearted?

The object I had seen in the pencil holder was still missing. I wished I could examine it again.

Suddenly I remembered that there should be a secret drawer in this desk. I found it quite easily. As I looked inside, I thought I would be sick. I leaned forward and rested my forehead on the cool polished wood of the desk. Then I looked back at the drawer. There was the fire-blackened object I had seen before. There was my cameo. And a diamond ring, no doubt the one Britt had given Lucy. There was nothing else in the drawer.

I picked up my cameo. At that moment I heard voices at the back door. Hastily I closed the drawer and moved away from the desk with the cameo clutched tightly in my hand.

Chapter 18

"Why, Tracy, I thought you were lying down," Alex said in surprise as they came into the office. "Should she be up, Chris?"

"If she feels like it. How *do* you feel, Tracy?"

"I have a headache, but otherwise I'm all right." I thought of the nausea I'd felt a few moments ago, but I didn't mention it since I knew it had nothing to do with my physical condition.

The sheriff came forward, hitching the belt over his fat stomach and mopping his face with a handkerchief. His voice sounded irritable, as if he resented the bother we were being to him. "I want to talk to Miss Meadows. Then I'll get a statement from the rest of you, just to know where you all were at the time."

"Will you need me again?" Jim asked.

"No, I think you've pretty well covered everything. If you think of anything you forgot, be sure to call and let me know."

"I'll run you home, Jim," Alex said. "It's too dark to walk."

The sheriff sat down behind Alex's desk and looked at me. I told him what had happened, being as concise and coherent as I could. When I finished, he took a folded sheet of typewriter paper from his shirt pocket, smoothed it out, and handed it to me. "Did you write this?"

Dear Alex,
The little dog laughed, but I am going to jump over the moon. You come with me. The sun is hot in July. We will have a picnic, you and Elizabeth and I. I like her. The roses are blood red. Come soon.

Love,
Tracy

"This doesn't make sense," I said.

"Did you write it?"

I handed the paper back to him. "No, of course not. It's crazy."

"People who commit suicide *are* crazy, Miss Meadows," the sheriff said, watching me. His eyes were opaque but shiny; they looked like dark wet pebbles. I didn't say anything. I knew what he was thinking. He didn't believe someone had tried to kill me. He thought, like the rest, that I had attempted suicide.

"Lots of people who commit suicide leave notes," he said. "They don't make such good sense sometimes, but you can always see a purpose in them. To ask for forgiveness. Or to make a confession. This one puzzles me. I don't see any reason behind it."

No reason behind it. They had convinced him I was crazy. Next he would ask me about the ghost.

"Where did you find the note?" I asked.

"Over there in the typewriter." He nodded toward the typing table on the far wall. I stared at the typewriter. Its keyboard looked like a grinning mouth full of white teeth. I felt hopeless. Not Alex, I thought again. Let it be anybody but Alex.

The sheriff asked, "What are you thinking, Miss Meadows? Who wrote the note?"

"I don't know."

"You looked as if you did. You could see through this door as you went to the garage. Was someone in here then?"

Alex, I thought. Alex was the only person in the house. The typewriter belonged to Alex, and he was the only person who ever used it. I said, "No, I saw no one. Alex and I had talked in here when I first came in, but that was some time before I left."

"He says he went for a walk right after you talked. Can you corroborate that?"

Hope flared. Perhaps it was true; perhaps he had gone for a walk. The house had been so silent. Because no one was in it? I didn't know. "Surely you can't suspect Alex," I said.

"I suspect everybody, Miss Meadows. I like Alex, and he's an important man in Abbeville. But

I'm sworn to uphold the law, and as far as I'm concerned no one is above suspicion."

"You believe me," I said surprised.

"Believe someone tried to kill you? Yes, I do. The note is too crazy. Also, I've never seen a suicide where the person knocked himself in the head. Someone tried to kill you, and he may try again."

"Yes, I know that."

"You meant to spend the night with Sandra Parker, Alex said. I think you ought to go ahead with your plans."

"No, not now," I said.

Somehow it had come to me in the past hour that I could not leave Wisteria. Before, I would have been running from some unknown force, some mysterious power of evil. But now I would be running from my own suspicions. If it were Alex trying to destroy me, what was the good of running? To believe him guilty would be as destructive as losing my life. Without Alex I had no life.

As I started out, the sheriff said, "Oh, Miss Meadows, I meant to tell you. I haven't found your cameo. But I'm still working on it."

I was hotly conscious of the cameo clutched in my hand, and I wondered if he could read my face. "All right," I mumbled and went hurriedly down the hall.

Alex was not yet back from Jim's. When I entered the living room, Britt solicitously seated me on the sofa. He asked, "What did Mr. Bridges say? Does he know who's guilty?"

"He didn't tell me. He wants to see you one at a time." I looked around at them, at their faces still excited and bright with curiosity. I knew they had been talking about what happened, going over and around it from every angle. Now they wanted me to join their discussion. But suddenly I did not want to talk about it any longer.

"I think I'll go to my room," I said. "Maybe after a night's sleep I'll feel better."

"Would you like me to go with you?" Pam asked.

"No, thank you, I'll be fine."

I walked slowly up the stairs. My feet were leaden; it was an effort to pick them up. I seemed to be moving through a thick fog. The ticking of the clock in the upper hall was muffled and slow; it seemed to come from a great distance. My hand hurt. I saw that I was still holding tightly to the cameo, and I put it in the silver case. I began to undress slowly with long pauses when I forgot what I was to do next. At last I dropped into bed and fell into a heavy sleep.

I woke several hours later in a thick still darkness. No night birds called; no frogs croaked; no insects buzzed and fluttered. Disturbed by the silence, I got up quietly and moved across the room to the windows. Looking out, I saw that the sky was starless and moonless, covered by low-hanging clouds.

A small scraping sound on the wooden floor of the sun deck made my neck tingle. I moved across the carpeted floor in my bare feet, making no sound, and looked through the French doors. Someone was on the sun deck, standing at the bannisters and looking over them to the terrace. Even in the darkness I recognized the outline of those broad thick shoulders. It was Alex!

I jumped back, instinctively wishing to keep him from seeing me. What was he doing there? He turned and looked toward the door, toward me, but he could not see me, hidden as I was by the draperies. I watched him as he moved all the way around the railing, apparently looking below. Then he started toward the door. I wanted to scream, wake the rest of the house, bring someone to my rescue. But I could not. I knew I would make no sound. I would wait for him silently and put up no struggle. I had no defenses against him. Even as I saw him come toward the door I could not believe it was Alex who would harm me, Alex who wanted me dead.

He stopped not two feet from me with only a glass door and a length of fabric between us. His hand was on the knob. In the lightning flash of memory one sometimes gets in extreme danger, I remembered that I had not locked the door before going to bed. In my heavy tiredness it had been all I could do to get undressed. On this one night I had not locked the door, and soon he would open it.

But he didn't. He stood for a few seconds with his hand on the knob, and then he turned and went swiftly across the deck and down the stairs to the terrace.

I stood staring at the empty sun deck. I felt deathly ill.

Chapter 19

I woke to the sound of rain on the roof, swift hard spatters interspersed with moments of silence. The sky was low and gray with rough angry clouds racing about. Wind spasmodically rattled the windows. I snuggled down into the covers, but soon I threw them back. It was difficult to tell whether I was hot or cold. The air seemed heavy and unsettled; even the wind and rain came in jerky bursts, as if unable to decide what to do.

A knock sounded on my door, and I called, "Who is it?"

"Alex. I just wanted to tell you I'm going to bring your breakfast up in a few minutes."

I put on my yellow robe, brushed my teeth, and gingerly combed my hair, being careful of the sore spot. Just as I finished, Alex knocked again and came in carrying a loaded silver tray, which he put on a small table beside the windows. Then he turned to me. "How do you feel this morning? Any effects from last night?"

"The lump is still there, but it doesn't hurt except when I touch it. I'm fine." But I did not meet his eyes.

He took my face in his hands. "I worried about you all night," he said. "In fact, I prowled around most of the night, trying to be sure nothing else happened to you. I was tempted to wake you to talk, but I decided you needed your sleep."

So that was why Alex was on the sun deck: to guard me from harm. He had come toward the door thinking to wake me. I felt a hundred pounds lighter, as if gravity had released its hold on me. "Let's eat," I said. "I'm hungry."

"First, let me turn on some lights. There's too much blue in this room. It isn't my favorite color at best, and today it's downright gloomy."

"I thought men always liked blue," I said.

"Perhaps I'm prejudiced against it because I associate it with Myra."

I was startled. "But I thought—that is, you always seemed so fond of her."

"Until recently I didn't realize I wasn't. Oh, I knew I couldn't love her no matter how convenient a marriage between us would have been. However, we got through that period without any hard feelings. It was only the loneliness of widowhood that made her turn to me; she said as much herself afterward . . . But lately I've begun to see what she is doing to Pam and Britt, possessively holding them, crippling their lives. I've watched her belittle you in a dozen subtle ways. I think she caused most of our quarrels. She's a devil, Tracy."

"I don't know," I said slowly. "She was kind to me the night Grandfather was sick. And I keep remembering how fond of her Pam is."

He hardly seemed to hear what I said. He was thinking of something else. "I don't think we can ever be happy at Wisteria with Myra here. I must think of some way to get her to leave. There should be somewhere she would like to go."

"To Europe," I said, remembering Myra's barely concealed envy of the couple who had just returned.

"Of course. Why didn't I think of that? It's just the thing—glamorous and exciting and with plenty of details to manage."

"She'll meet some new men," I said. "Beautiful as she is, she'll probably find someone to marry."

Happily, we planned the trip—for Myra, piling detail on detail. I almost forget all the other problems at Wisteria in my joy at getting this big one settled. I was glad to know too that Alex wasn't blind and uncaring, as I had sometimes thought. He had seen how Myra was treating me and resented it.

We fell silent when Myra knocked and stuck her head in the door. "Pam told me you were up here," she said, glancing at my robe with narrowed eyes. "I thought you might have forgotten the time. We'll need to leave for church soon."

"We aren't going," Alex said. "I don't think

Tracy should after her ordeal last night, and I'm going to stay with her."

"Oh," she said, "are you feeling worse, Tracy? Shall I call Chris?"

"No, she's fine," Alex said. "The rest of you go ahead to church."

She hesitated. I thought she was unwilling to leave me alone with Alex; she would have liked to stay at home with us, listening to our conversation, nurturing every tiny disagreement between us. But after another look at Alex, she closed the door and went away.

"I'll go downstairs and let you get dressed," Alex said. "We'll sit primly in the living room and read the papers while they're gone."

"Not in the living room," I said with a smile. "It's blue, too."

"You're going to have to make some changes around here later. All right, the library. It's strange how much I'm looking forward to spending an hour with you. But do you realize how little time we've had together since we came here? I've missed you, Tracy."

We were both standing up. He put his arms around me and kissed me. Then he let me go and said, "Enough of that. There'll be no scandal for us, young lady. I'm getting out of here right now." He picked up the tray and went.

I too was looking forward to the hour when the rest of the family would be at church and Alex and I alone in the house. We would sit primly reading the paper, he said. But we could talk, too, and get some of our other problems settled.

But when I got downstairs, Britt was in the library with Alex. "Hello, Tracy. Feeling better this morning?"

"Much better." I paused. "Aren't you going to church?"

"No, I ache all over, as if I were taking a cold. It's probably nothing, but I don't want to take a chance. Summer colds are always the worst kind."

"I'm sorry," I said automatically. I *was* sorry, but mostly because I was so disappointed at not being able to talk to Alex freely. We were getting along so well upstairs. Now that we were communicating at last, I'd hoped we could solve the mysteries which were keeping us apart. Now my time with Alex was spoiled.

But to my surprise, Britt left us. "You two must have a lot to talk about," he said. "I'll be in the living room if you want me. Mind if I take the sports section?"

While Alex and I talked about the news of the day, I cast about in my mind for a way to bring up the subject of the cameo. There seemed no tactful way to tell him I had found it in his drawer. "Alex," I said, "I found my cameo last night."

I could discern no guilt or embarrassment on his face, nothing but astonishment. "You did! Where?"

"In the secret drawer of your desk."

"The what?"

"The secret drawer. With the other things, the letter sealer, or whatever it is, and Lucy's diamond ring."

The astonishment on his face was turning into

something else, something that quite frightened me. "I don't know what you are talking about," he said. "I don't know about any secret drawer. And I certainly haven't had your cameo or a diamond ring—Lucy's you said?"

"Yes. Britt told me it disappeared the weekend she spent here."

"Well, good God, I didn't take it," he exploded. "I didn't even know it was gone."

I said slowly, "Then someone else is using your secret drawer. Who knows about it?"

"How should I know? I wasn't even aware of it myself." He thought a minute. "Myra might have known. She bought the desk at an antique shop. I told you the original furniture was missing when she redecorated the room."

"Then she must have stolen my cameo. And Lucy's diamond."

He frowned. "It's hard to believe. She might have envied you, but she's no thief. I can't see— yes, I can, too. Stealing the ring broke up Britt's romance, and the loss of the cameo put a strain on ours. She must have planned—"

The telephone rang in the hall. "I'll get it," Britt called. A moment later he came to the door. "Somebody called and said a fence is down over near Cedar Creek and he doesn't want your cows in his fields."

Alex got up. "I'll have to go."

"It's raining again," I protested.

"Farm work can't wait for good weather. I'll be back as soon as I can." He got up and started out.

"I'd offer to go with you except for this cold," Britt said.

"You better not go out," Alex answered. "I can probably handle it myself. If not, I'll get Jim to help."

I walked to the window and stood looking out at the slanting rain. Alex's pickup came down the drive, and I waved to him. I couldn't tell if he looked my way; he was only a dark huddled shape sitting high on the seat of the pickup.

Alex would come home tired and wet and chilled. If we were married, I would go out to the kitchen and make some hot chocolate. We would drink it at a table with a red-checked cloth, happy to be cozily inside together.

"This is tornado weather," Britt said.

"What?" I had to bring my thoughts back from the pleasant vision I had been contemplating. "Tornado weather? How can you tell?"

"I heard it on the radio early this morning. Tornado warnings all day, they said. But I would have known anyway from the clouds."

"I don't see anything special about them."

"When you've lived all your life in tornado country, you learn. Tornado clouds are dark gray or black, and they look bottom-heavy. Sometimes they are horn-shaped wisps hanging toward the ground."

"I don't see anything like that."

He came to the window. Suddenly he seemed quite excited. "We've got to get to the storm cellar in a hurry," he said.

"The clouds don't look any worse to me than they did early this morning."

"They are though. There's going to be a storm." He took my hand. "Come on. We'll be safe in the cellar."

He pulled me into the hall and toward the back door. "It's raining, Britt," I protested. "What about your cold? I don't think there's a storm. Shouldn't we turn on the radio?"

"Tracy, don't be a fool," he cried. "There isn't time. Come on. Hurry!" Even as he spoke, he was running down the hall, pulling me along beside him. Seeing his white face, I began to be frightened. I ran faster. Hatless and coatless, we slammed out the back door and into the rain. In a moment I was soaked through. It seemed a long way. Why had they built the storm cellar so far from the house? I wondered if we would be in time. Even now one of those hornlike clouds might be swooping down.

We dashed down the concrete steps, and Britt pushed the door open. I caught my breath and looked around. It was a small concrete room about nine by twelve, empty except for a round white water heater in one corner and one solitary paint bucket in another.

"There used to be some folding chairs," Britt said. "They must be upstairs. I'll dash up and get two."

"No, Britt," I cried.

But I was too late; he had already gone, slamming the door behind him. It was dark with the door closed; only a very dim light came through a transom above the door. There must be a light switch somewhere, probably just inside the door. My groping hands found the switch and clicked it, but nothing happened. The electricity was off. The storm must have blown down a line.

Britt should be back by now. I wished he would come back. I fumbled for the doorknob. How difficult to be without sight. How did blind people manage? Finally I found it. The door wouldn't open!

I turned the knob again and pulled with all my might. Refusing to accept what my mind told me, I kept struggling to get the door open, twisting the knob, knocking against the door with my shoulder. I couldn't believe it was locked. It hadn't been when we came. I pounded on the door and called him. But I got no answer.

Suddenly I smelled gas. I stopped my pounding and heard a hissing sound like a boiling teakettle. The water heater! I groped my way toward it, trying to think of where the cutoff would be. I hadn't paid much attention to the heater when we came in. All I remembered was that it was white and cylindrical. We had a similar one in the laundry room of the dormitory at college. That one had a little door at the bottom where the flame was, and by the door was a knob that presumably turned off the gas. I hoped this one was the same.

It seemed even darker than before; the blackness was almost complete. I couldn't find the heater. I looked around for the transom, hoping to get my bearings by it. The transom had disappeared! For a moment I was panic-stricken and completely disoriented. Then high on one wall I discerned a faint difference in the blackness. The transom was still there, but it was now so dark outside that I had not been able to see it at first.

The water heater would be in the right hand corner of the room. Finally I found it, ran my hands down its smooth sides to the bottom, and located the cutoff. I gasped in surprise.

I sat down on the concrete floor. The gas was not on. Yet I could hear it and smell it. Where could it be coming from? There must be a leak in the pipes. Panic fluttered my heart. I didn't know what to do. I couldn't find the leak, and even if I did, I wouldn't be able to fix it. If only Britt would come back!

Suddenly my heart stilled. He wasn't coming back. Something had happened to him. He had been hurt in the storm. Or had something else harmed him, something unnatural and evil? Something that had tried to kill me twice, something that could overcome any human protection.

I shivered, and the involuntary shaking brought back some of my common sense. Escaping gas had nothing to do with the supernatural. I was still alive. I wasn't beaten yet.

I moved away from the heater, to the corner diagonally across from it, thinking perhaps the gas would not be so strong there. Air, my mind was shouting, get some air. The transom. But it was too high; there was no way to reach it. There was nothing in the room but the water heater. And, I suddenly remembered, the paint bucket. My heart sank as I looked toward the transom. It was so high. Still, it seemed my only chance. I groped my way to the corner and picked up the bucket. Metal banged against concrete. I had knocked something over. I groped on the floor. My hand closed over a rectangular metal can, possibly a turpentine can, I thought as I heard a liquid sloshing. It was too small to be of any use. I set it down and found the paint bucket again.

Standing on the paint bucket, I strained to reach the transom. Thankfulness washed over me as I felt my fingers touch the bottom frame. I felt for the catch. Frantically, I felt again. I wanted to cry. How stupid I was. There was no catch at the bottom. The transom opened from the top. Desperately, I strained to reach higher. If I could ram my fist through the glass—I would be cut, but what of that? A cut was nothing. It would bleed though. Perhaps I should not be able to get it stopped. My life would spurt out on this concrete floor.

I forced the fearful pictures from my mind. I had to have air. Without it I would die. The memory of my black pain in the swimming pool washed over me. I would do anything—anything—to get air. I drove my fist toward the glass. It hit on the wooden frame. Pain jarred through me. I drew my arm back again, bent my knees, and jumped as high as I could. My fist dragged down the concrete wall as I fell. It was scraped raw and bleeding. It was no use. I was not tall enough; the paint bucket was too small; I could not reach the glass.

If I could throw the bucket—It was unwieldy, but—Suddenly I remembered the turpentine can. It was small, yet heavy enough to throw forcibly. I found it, drew back my arm to throw. I had been a pretty fair basketball player at school. Dear Lord, let me hit that transom, I prayed.

I heard the blessed crack of the glass, the tinkle of the pieces as they fell to the floor. Suddenly there was a bigger noise, like a jet engine on the lawn outside. My skirt pulled tight against my legs behind and billowed out in front as the air rushed out of the room to fill the storm-created vacuum outside. Then with a whoosh something light and wet showered down on me. I brushed frantically until I realized the objects were wet leaves.

The gas smell was hardly noticeable now; the storm had taken out the foul air and given me fresh. But the gas was still escaping, and the storm was gone. I wondered if one opening would give me enough air to survive until someone found me.

I wondered, too, what was happening outside. I conjured up a picture of Britt pinned down by storm wreckage, bleeding, his face white and twisted with pain. Of Wisteria destroyed, its chimneys standing bleak among the debris. Of Alex returning to the scene, seeking me in panic.

If only I could get out of here. But the door and the transom were the only openings, and neither of them was any use to me. I could only wait, imagining the scene that would meet my eyes when someone finally found me.

Yet perhaps my mental pictures were all wrong. Perhaps it wasn't an accident that kept Britt from returning. Someone could have fixed the pipe, knowing that sooner or later the opportunity would come to use it. Then seeing us go in, he could have prevented Britt's return, locked the door, and turned on the gas to kill me.

Immediately I could see the faults in my reasoning. It took time for a room to fill up with gas. The family would return from church. Alex would come back from his fence mending. I would be missed. Britt, unless he were dead, would tell them where I was. How could the murderer know I wouldn't be found in time?

Would I be found in time? The smell of gas was growing stronger again. I was wet still, and my hand hurt dreadfully. But none of that mattered as long as I could breathe. I looked toward the transom and saw that it was lighter outside now. I could see the jagged edges of glass where the can had gone through. Air was coming through that hole, I reminded myself. But I did not know whether it would be enough to sustain me. There was no way to call for help. There was no one out there anyway except Britt, and he was hurt, perhaps dead. Now he would never be the richest man in the state—

My thoughts stopped. Suddenly everything fell into place. I knew who wanted me dead and why. Scenes flashed before my eyes, click, click, click, like a rapidly moving slide projector. I saw Britt's hand reaching for a twenty dollar bill and heard Alex say, "He's on his own now that I'm getting married." I saw Britt swimming near me in the pool, saw his face when Grandfather and Alex talked about the wills and my inheritance, saw him take the milk for Grandfather from my hand. I heard him suggest that I had attempted suicide. It was Britt who insisted we come to the storm cellar, dragging me along while I protested. Britt suggested getting the chairs, a foolish thing to do if he really thought a storm was coming. He had slammed the door; no doubt he had locked it, too.

Britt was accustomed to borrowing freely from Alex. He had expected to be Alex's heir. With me out of the way, he *would* be Alex's heir; he would have no trouble persuading Pam to forego her share as she had before. And, I suddenly realized, through Alex, Britt would be my heir, too. Even Grandfather's heir if Grandfather had died before me. Britt would get it all.

Only Britt could have made sure no one would find me in time. "She's in her room taking a nap," he could have said when the rest of the family returned. "She doesn't want to be disturbed."

Someone, Alex perhaps, might say, "I'll look in on her to be sure she is all right."

"She said she was going to lock her door," he would reply. "I can't blame her after all that has happened."

And the door would be locked, because he himself would have locked it. No one would try to wake me—at least not for several hours.

Perhaps there would even be another suicide note.

Yes, Britt could have managed it. Would have managed it, if he hadn't overlooked the turpentine can or failed to realize its possibilities.

Suddenly the faint far-off sound of shouting came to me through the hole in the transom. I couldn't understand the words or tell where they were coming from, but my heart leaped. The shouts grew fainter and soon died away. Long minutes passed. I strained every nerve to hear as I tried to guess what was going on outside.

Then I heard a crunching noise just below the transom. Someone was walking on the broken glass. I pounded on the door, crying "Help! Help!" The crunching noise came again, but nothing happened. I sank hopelessly to the floor. It was Britt coming to see if I was dead. Now he knew about the broken transom. What would he do? My head was aching cruelly, and my nose and throat burned. I couldn't fight any longer. It was hopeless anyway. I would die here. Britt would have his way, and no one would know. Life would go on as before. Britt's stores would prosper; perhaps one day he *would* be the richest man in the state. No one would ever know he was a murderer.

The door pushed inward, bringing a wave of fresh air. Myra bent over me and started to drag me out the door. But I said hoarsely, "I can walk."

Chapter 20

Sipping hot tea in the living room later, I thought how amazing it was that life could change in an hour, in a moment, yet the outward semblances remain the same. The living room was no different with its lovely antique furniture, the harmonious shades of blue and lavender, the omnipresent wisteria blossoms. The people looked the same. Alex's face was dark and brooding. Chris smoked silently and looked at Pam. Sandra stood at the window with her back to the room. Myra was knitting; her hands moved rapidly, and she did not look up. It could have been any afternoon at Wisteria.

Except that Britt was dead. His body was at the funeral home now, but it would be brought back to

Wisteria. Pam had suggested it, and after a moment Alex agreed. "He's dead now, so it doesn't matter," he said. "Let the dead rest in peace."

Already the family friends were making their gestures of aid and comfort. Jim and his sons were moving the furniture in the hall to make a place for the casket. Later they would show the callers where to park and keep things running smoothly until the funeral. Mrs. Gilbert and her daughters were here to accept the food brought by friends and neighbors and keep careful lists so that everyone could be thanked. Somebody was answering the telephone, tactfully keeping people away until we had time to collect ourselves. Someone else had gone to the hospital to get Grandfather.

I heard a car pull up to the door, and Grandfather came in. I went to meet him. He put an arm around my shoulder. "Thank God, you're all right," he said. He looked around the room. "All I've heard is that Britt was killed in the storm. How did it happen? Or do you know?"

"I saw it," Alex said. "Britt was going across the backyard toward the house in the rain. He was coming from the gas meter, but I didn't know that then. Suddenly the sky darkened to night, and then the black cloud swooshed down with a roar and rolled along the ground carrying away everything in its path. When it passed, the rain had stopped, but I could see no sign of Britt. A big swath was cut across the backyard and into the woods beyond. I jumped out of the truck and ran down the path of the storm, climbing over fallen trees. Britt's body was about a mile away."

"No one else was hurt?" Grandfather asked.

"No, Tracy was in the storm cellar, and everyone else was at church in town."

Grandfather turned his puzzled eyes to me. "Why wasn't Britt in the storm cellar, too?" he asked.

"He didn't know a storm was coming," Alex said. "There hadn't been any warnings on the radio—he was lying when he told Tracy that—and from the library he couldn't see the cloud building up. He couldn't have guessed nature would devise an ironic ending to the crime he planned."

"Britt tried to kill me, Grandfather," I said. "He insisted we go to the storm cellar, and then he locked me in and turned on the gas."

Alex said to Grandfather's shocked face, "It's true. We don't know when he disconnected the pipes. Perhaps early this morning, seeing that the unsettled weather would provide an excuse to lure Tracy out there. But he could have done it days before. The furnace isn't in use at this time of year, and the only other gas fixture is the water heater in the bathhouse. No one would have known the gas was off while he waited for the right moment. It was easy to get me out of the way; anyone can ring his own phone by dialing a code number. Later he would have said it was a crank call."

"Three times he tried to kill me," I said with a shiver. "And you, too, Grandfather. We think he put the sleeping pills in your milk when he took it up."

Grandfather nodded. "I guess he got them from you," he said to Chris.

Sandra spoke for the first time. She had gone to sit in a corner, her long face completely devoid of color, her gray eyes staring blindly. "No, he got the pills from me," she said. "I think he meant them for Tracy, because I missed them the day after she came. But I thought I had misplaced them. It was only after I got back to town and heard about your overdose, Mr. Meadows, that I put two and two together. I accused Britt, and we quarreled."

She paused and looked around. "I couldn't go to the police," she said apologetically. "I loved Britt. Anyway, I wasn't sure. But I felt Tracy was in danger, and the only thing I could think to do was get her away from Wisteria."

"Surely when we called you about Tracy's accident in the garage, you could have told us your suspicions," Alex said.

"But don't you see? That relieved my mind. I thought that couldn't have been Britt, because he had left the house. Don't you remember, Tracy? I told you he had gone to the store."

"He didn't though," Pam said. "Jim said no car left after Tracy got home."

"That was when he got in a hurry," Alex said. "Knowing Sandra was suspicious and Tracy was going to leave, he couldn't wait. He had to give up the possibility of getting Mr. Meadows's money.

"Wait a minute," I said. "The first time Britt tried to kill me, in the swimming pool, he didn't even know about my money or the wills. Could we be mistaken after all?"

"He didn't know about *your* money," Alex said, "but he knew I wouldn't give him any more of mine after I married. And he knew, or could guess, that he and Pam would no longer be my heirs. He determined to prevent the wedding from the very first."

I thought of that first night at Wisteria when Britt had hemmed me in and stood looking down at me. But I knew I would never tell Alex about that. Other thoughts, too, were better left unspoken, although I could not help thinking them. With me out of the way and so much money coming to Britt after Alex's death, would Alex have been safe? Had Britt even perhaps had something to do with the accident which killed Roy, his stepfather? No, I would never voice those thoughts.

Alex spoke again. "After the first attempt to kill you, he decided it was unnecessary. He overheard us quarreling—about Jim, don't you remember?—and thought we were on the verge of breaking up. So he ceased his efforts, played a waiting game. It was only after he found out about your money that he saw you had to die after all, and if possible, Mr. Meadows before you."

Alex paused a moment. Then he said thoughtfully, "The ironic thing is that he would have made his own fortune if he had been willing to wait. He had all the essential qualities—the ability to grab an opportunity, to make plans rapidly and carry them out boldly, to turn an existing situation to his advantage. As he did when he wrote the crazy note, using the ghost to provide motivation for your suicide."

"Using the ghost?" Chris asked. "You mean

Britt wasn't the ghost? Surely you aren't going to tell us it was real."

Alex looked at Myra. Color came up under her fair skin, but she met his eyes defiantly. Alex said, "That wasn't hard to figure out, Myra. As soon as I knew you stole the cameo, I remembered other things. You're an excellent dancer. You were the star of your ballet class in college, weren't you? So I knew it would have been easy for you to float and melt and do all the other things Tracy saw the ghost do. Don't deny it. I've already searched your room and found the black wig and the white dress."

Suddenly I remembered: Britt had searched Myra's room, too. No wonder I had felt he knew something about the ghost.

She lifted her chin. "What if I did try to scare Tracy? There was no real harm. I thought she would decide she didn't want to live at Wisteria and go away quietly. Everything I did—the ghost, the cameo, the wedding dress, the stories I made up, the quarrels I caused—they were only efforts to make Tracy leave."

She paused. "Tracy was about to catch me near the swimming pool that night. I was wearing black leotards under the white dress, so I sank to the ground, ripped the dress off, and crawled into the nearby bushes. I was scared to death she wouldn't be taken in by the illusion I was trying to create. Don't you see why I went to so much trouble? It was all for you, to keep you from making an unsuitable marriage."

"Lucy was unsuitable, too," Pam said slowly.

"Well, she was. I'm not sorry I stopped the marriage by taking her ring. It wasn't stealing. I never would have worn it or sold it. It has been right there in Alex's desk all this time."

"Along with the other things," I said. I would never mention the branding iron now that I knew it for what it was, a mere stage prop to make her stories seem more believable.

"Don't you see?" she said again, her eyes resting on Alex and then Pam. "Everything I did was for your own good."

"Even keeping me here at Wisteria," Pam said. She looked at Chris and said slowly, "We've decided to buy the Evans place and move immediately."

"No!" Myra said in a cracked voice. "No, you can't. Not now. Not with Britt gone, too." I thought she was on the verge of tears, Myra, who was always perfectly self-possessed. I felt sorry for her. She had been unkind to me in many ways, but I thought she loved Britt and Pam as she understood love. Britt had turned out to be a murderer and was dead, and Pam was leaving. Myra had nothing left.

"Things can't stay the same, Myra," Alex said. "You'll have to make your own life somewhere else. I thought perhaps you might like to go to Europe."

"But that's impossible. There are so many things to be taken care of here. The storm damage and—" she stopped. "But I guess Tracy will do that." For a moment she looked utterly lost. I saw Grandfather's eyes on her speculatively, and I thought, Oh, no.

"I have to go to Paris next month," he said. "Maybe you'll be going about the same time?"

I watched Myra's face, saw the realization dawn on her that Grandfather was still a handsome man —and a rich one. I was worried, but I said nothing. I would not try to manage other people's lives as Myra had.

Gradually the room emptied. Grandfather was the last to go. As he started out, Alex stopped him. "Mr. Meadows, I feel I should warn you," he said awkwardly. "It's about Myra. She is selfish and scheming and possessive. She latches on and won't let go. I'd hate to see you in her clutches."

Grandfather smiled wickedly. "Beautiful women have been clutching at me for thirty years, Alex. But I just may let Myra catch me. I think she would keep me alive twenty years past my time if she thought the money stopped when I died."

Alex looked surprised, and I laughed. "I was worried about you a moment ago, Grandfather. But I see you can take care of yourself with Myra."

After Grandfather left, Alex turned to me. "Tracy, I'd like to go for a walk before the callers start. Do you feel like coming with me?"

We said nothing important on that walk. All the big important things had been settled. They were over, finished. We would not think of them again soon. Later perhaps we would talk of them, telling how we felt in such and such an instance and why we acted as we did. Now it was enough that it was over and we were together. We spoke of the house and the garden and how soon we could be married.

When we finally came back, the hearse was standing before the front door. It had brought Britt's body back, and Wisteria stood waiting to receive it. Remembering my feelings the first time I saw the house and knowing I would live here the rest of my life, I raised my eyes to it fearfully. But it was just a house, graceful and well-kept. Its white paint glistened in the late afternoon sunlight; its windows gleamed; the red brick chimneys rose tall and straight as the day they were made. But it had no life or personality of its own. It would shelter its occupants against the weather and provide a space for their lives to be played out, but it could do no more. It could neither comfort nor sadden. It could not protect against evil, but neither could it create it. It was just a house, a pile of inanimate bricks and wood, waiting for whatever emotions its occupants would put in it. As Alex had once said, we would fill it with love, so much love there would be room for nothing else.

Even the wisteria blooms, which I had thought a symbol of grief, had no power over me now. For I saw them not as the whole of Wisteria but as an essential part. Life has much grief in it, but it has gladness, too. I could accept both.

Hand in hand we walked toward Wisteria together.

A Guide to Making It Big on Capitol Hill!
THE GIRLS OF WASHINGTON by David Brown
(nationally syndicated cartoonist of Today's World)
$1.25

SEND TO: BELMONT TOWER BOOKS
P.O. Box 2050
Norwalk, Connecticut 06852

Please send me _____ copy(s) of THE GIRLS OF WASHINGTON, BT 50997. In enclose $ _____ in cash, check, or money order. Please add 35¢ handling fee per copy. Order five or more copies and we will pay for shipping. Sorry, no C.O.D.'s.

For orders outside U.S. add $1.00 for the first book and 25¢ for each additional title.

NAME _____
(Please print)
ADDRESS _____
CITY _____ STATE _____ ZIP _____

Allow 4 Weeks for Delivery

THE ORGANIZATION   BT50546   95¢
A.D. Brent

Johnny Merak was out for revenge against THE ORGANIZATION. Before it was over, either Merak would be dead or the crime bosses would be behind bars. Here is the inside story of how an underworld organization had an entire city in the grips of its rapacious tentacles. "Things like this can't happen in America." Says who?

THE RINGER   BT50766 $1.25
Dell Shannon

A Luis Mendoza mystery by top crime writer Dell Shannon. LAPD Detective Lieutenant Mendoza has to face the possibility that a fellow cop and good friend is the brains behind a stolen car ring. His search for the truth takes him from back alleys to Beverly Hills mansions. "Another great case book from Dell Shannon"—*L.A. Times*.

MURDER WITH LOVE   BT50775 $1.25
Dell Shannon

The earthquake rocked Los Angeles and was followed by the wildest outbreak of crime in the city's history. Mendoza was assigned to get to the bottom of things.

MAN ALONE   BT50776 $1.25
E.H. Manring

Steve Douglas could have walked away and let the Mafia goons take over his ranch. The mob had the guns and the most vicious contract killers money could buy, but this once they had taken on the wrong man!

MOBSTER   BT50786 $1.25
Frank Arrigio

The true to life story of the rise of a tough East Side punk to a power crazed crime czar.

THE MEMOIRS OF SHERLOCK HOLMES
Sir Arthur Conan Doyle

BT50846 $1.25

A superb collection of the greatest detective stories ever written. Sir Arthur Conan Doyle is a master story teller and his hero, the immortal Sherlock Holmes, epitomizes the analytical mind. This volume includes "The Yellow Face," "The Musgrave Ritual," and "The Final Problem," Holmes' famous encounter with the evil genius, Moriarty.

THE RETURN OF SHERLOCK HOLMES
Sir Arthur Conan Doyle

BT50866 $1.25

For ten years Holmes was seen no more in Baker Street. Then in 1903 Doyle took pity on his readers and brought the remarkable sleuth back to life. The stories in this marvelous book tell of his return. Like Holmes himself, they are immortal.

PIMP
Peter Whitfield

BT50885 $1.50

He was big time and into big money and he meant to keep it that way. This is the story of a New York pimp, brutal and streetwise, an operator who makes more money than the President of the United States. Told in his own words, this is a chronicle of street crime at its worst.

BLOODY SUNDAY
Frank Scarpetta

BT50909 $1.25

Magellan set out to pay back the old woman who had nursed him back to health and saved his life. Her grandchild, a beautiful young girl, had been brutally murdered. It had the stink of the Mafia about it and Magellan was going to see that they paid the full price—death.